Leather and Lillies

Inflamed Flowers, Volume 2

Amie Taylor

Published by Amie Taylor, 2024.

LEATHER AND LILLIES

First edition. July 6, 2024.

Copyright © 2024 Amie Taylor.

ISBN: 979-8227694294

Written by Amie Taylor.

1

Bailey stood backstage at the Sweet Treasures strip club in Los Angeles, California, thinking how much her life had changed these past two years. It all started her second year in college, that one spring break when her dearest friend had been kidnapped by her father. Nothing had been the same since that one fateful day, which changed her life forever and destroyed all she ever was. She grabbed a joint from her purse and lit it; slowly, she brought it up to her trembling lips. The moment she inhaled the smoke, all her memories of that spring flowed back into her head. They hit her like a lightning bolt and then came all the pain and loneliness she had with these memories. Bailey remembered when she first met her beloved friend. Kaitlyn was a sweet, innocent girl who knew nothing of life or love. They instantly become friends, Bailey taking her under her wing. Kaitlyn was everything she had not been, so damn innocent, so pure, where she was very blunt and wild, untamable. Perhaps this was why she had befriended her so easily, so quickly.

Bailey laughed softly, remembering the day she had introduced Kaitlyn to Jax, the lead singer of the band Seeds of Sorrow. Kaitlyn's eyes lit up like a frightened child as she saw what a real man looked like, a man fully experienced in the ways between a woman and a man. One who could give her pleasure beyond anything she had ever experienced before.in her sheltered life. It was Jax who had saved Kaitlyn from her deranged father. Even now, Bailey wished with all her heart that she would have gone with him. She expected Jax and Kaitlyn to show back to the dorms after he saved her. She expected them to tell her all about what had happened, but all she received was a short phone call that she would never forget.

"Bailey, Kaitlyn had said, I'm fine. My father will never hurt me again. I'm with Jax. I'll always love you, my friend. Goodbye."

Then, that was the last time she had spoken to her friend. Over the months that followed the phone call that cost her everything, Bailey lost all interest in her college studies. She missed Kaitlyn with every fiber of her being. She was so angry with her for walking out on her like she did with no explanation. She knew she could have gone to a Seeds of Sorrow concert and would more than likely see her. She could not bring herself to do it; she did not want to know the man from her past who was also lost to her forever, Nick, the band's drummer. Even more than this, she feared she would not be wanted in their lives. Desperate to find some peace within herself, she tried to move back home with her folks. They turned her away when they learned she had dropped out of college.

Tears fell from Bailey's eyes as she remembered how she struggled these past two years until she finally got a job as an exotic dancer here at Sweet Treasures. Sure, she knew it was not the most respected of jobs, but at least she wasn't a hooker. With this thought, she stood up and walked to her dressing room table. She glanced into her mirror. Tonight, she wore a red velvet corset with feathers around the bottom, revealing the mounds of her round, perky breasts. It barely covered her round, firm bottom; with it, she wore red fishnet pantyhose that stopped at her thighs, her red platforms that made her seem even taller than she already was. She wore her blond hair in a sloppy, loose bun with tiny ringlets hanging seductively around her luscious neck and chin. She smiled wickedly at her reflection, thinking that tonight she would get many tips for this little number. She finished off her look with deep red lipstick that stood out against her pale, milky-like skin.

"Legs, Legs, Legs," the screaming of the men outside the club got Bailey's attention. It was finally her turn to dance. She stood behind the stage curtain, waiting for her music to start, closing her eyes, and trying to drown out their shouts, yet she could still hear them. They all chanted her name repeatedly, thousands of men who lusted for her but would never love her. The realization made it easier for her to lose herself to the music and give them what they wanted to see but never give them more.

Hearing her music finally start, Bailey ran out onto the stage, grabbing the pole to give her body a twirl around it; she dropped and popped for all the men to see her luscious body and how she could shake it. Out in the spotlight, she was a million miles away, letting the echoes of the music fill her ears so she would not hear all the filthy comments coming from the men in her audience. She could not wait to get this night over with so she could drown herself in a whiskey bottle and forget all her misery and intense shame. She danced to the beat, her muscles became slick with sweat, and she danced away her painful, meaningless existence.

Later that evening, she sat at the bar in the club. Bailey had just finished her fourth shot of whiskey. Many times, several men had approached her, trying to pay her for sex; she tried to pretend that it was nothing, that it didn't bother her. However, it did on the inside she just wanted to explode, scream, and shout that she was not a whore. She wanted to slap those filthy pigs in their dirty mouths. She was so tired of never getting any respect. She wanted desperately to just say the hell with it all, walk out of that damn club and never come back. The problem was that she knew she had nowhere else to go. Instead of reacting less appropriately, she took another three shots of whiskey and walked away. She needed to get home to her hotel room, go to bed, and let sleep take her over, seizing all her thoughts.

2

Kaitlyn sat backstage in Arras, France, with her one-year-old son, Tristen Jax, in her arms. He was the most adorable, precious baby in the world, and he had her wrapped around his tiny little finger. The fact that he had the same enchanting emerald-green eyes as his father and the same devious grin made it much harder not to spoil him. There was not one inch of Tristen that resembled her. He was one hundred percent Jax from those eyes and that smile to his wavy blonde hair and light ghostly complexion. He would be tall like his father, already two inches taller than the other children his age. Jax told Kaitlyn many times that he could have had their son by himself, judging by the looks of him.

Kaitlyn smiled now, thinking of how good Jax was with their son, always giving him unconditional love and attention no matter how busy he was. He was a wonderful father to their boy and a fantastic lover to her. Lover, she hated this word. She wished they could get married, but the cold, hard fact was they could never be married because she left her identity behind two years ago when the man that she thought was her father tried to kill her. Standing up and walking across the room to lay Tristen in his crib, she decided it did not matter because she knew Jax loved her, and it would have to be enough. She laid her son down, leaned into the crib, and kissed him on his cheek, looking up at his nanny, who stood patiently by and smiled.

"Can you please be sure to keep a close eye on him for a few hours while I go see Jax," Kaitlyn asked. The nanny nodded yes, and Kaitlyn turned and padded out of the room.

Jax stood leaning against the wall, waiting for Kaitlyn to return from putting their son down for the night. Even after being with her every night for the past two years, he still wanted her with a desire that burned his soul. He could never touch or taste her enough to satisfy him; she was the fuel that set the fire. The light that saved him from the darkness of his life and soul. He smiled at her now, his eyes full of love and desire as he watched her mouth twist up in a smile of sheer passion.

The look on Jax's face as she entered the room took Kaitlyn's breath away. She had been with him long enough to know what he was thinking just by the look in his eyes, and right now, they twinkled, giving them a luminous glow. A smile curved across his firm lips; she knew instantly what he wanted. He wanted to kiss, touch, and taste her, and she could hardly wait. She slowly walked over to him as he held his hand out to hers, biting her lower lip, knowing full well how those strong hands felt upon her naked flesh.

Jax looked at Kaitlyn in raw desire, his shaft already hardening against his pants. He swore she got sexier with each passing day, especially after having their son. Her once slim body was shaped with very tempting curves, and her perky breasts were fuller yet still firm. The red dress she wore tonight clung to her tightly, showing off every one of those sexy curves. Wanting her with a fire that threatened to burn his very soul, he grabbed her, pulling her into his arms; her breasts slid across his broad chest seductively, causing his body to ache for her even more.

Kaitlyn's body trembled all over as Jax's mouth and tongue tasted the flesh of her neck and shoulders. His hands roamed over her back as his lips continued to explore her neck and shoulders, then her throat. She dropped her head back and arched upward toward him. His erection prodded against her through the fabric of her dress, and her knees weakened with desire. His strong hand slid down further to explore between her thighs, sliding up her skirt to stop at the honeyed patch of hair between them. His hand caressed her there very slowly, very gently; she moaned as bolts of electrifying pleasure shot through her body. She desperately wanted to feel those fingers inside of her taunting her, teasing her until she begged him to end the sweet torture on her tender body. He must have sensed what she wanted, for he now slowly thrust those fingers deep inside of her. Lord, help me, she thought; his fingers felt so good.

Kaitlyn almost exploded with passion right then and there as Jax continued this assault on her senses. She ran her hands through his hair and pulled his head up to kiss him on his firm lips, slowly letting them gently trail across his cheek. She whispered in his ear. "Jax, take me to our bed. Make love to me."

Without another word spoken between them, Jax swiftly pulled Kaitlyn into his arms and took her as she requested; once there, he undressed her, watching every inch of her soft body become revealed, removing her clothing piece by piece. After she was completely nude, he laid her gently back onto the bed where she could watch him undress. He loved seeing the desire that burned in her eyes each time she saw him naked. He loved that she craved his touch just as severely as he craved hers. Free of his clothes at last, Jax climbed over to Kaitlyn and parted her thighs with his knees. In one solid, savage thrust, he buried his throbbing shaft into her moist, eager body.

"Jax, you feel so good inside of me; make me feel so alive, so complete," Kaitlyn cried repeatedly.

Jax smiled at Kaitlyn's passionate spoken words, nibbling at her taunt nipples with his teeth, causing her to wither beneath him. He loved how she was finally over her shyness when they made love. She wasn't afraid to ask if she wanted him to give her pleasure in a certain way. She was no longer afraid to get a bit rough in her passion, cry out, and beg him for more. These thoughts escaped his mind after feeling Kaitlyn's hand frantically rummaging through his hair. He knew she was coming close to ecstasy. He rolled over, his cock still buried inside her ho sheath, pulling her on top of him.

"Ride me, my love; show me how much you want me to remain buried within you," he demanded.

Kaitlyn ran her hands down the muscles of Jax's chest, her nails raking across his tender flesh as she rode him gently. His hands gripped her hips, urging her to move faster, hard upon his throbbing erection. She watched his face as she began to move back and forth on top of his thick shaft. It was full of desire and pleasure, proving he loved every move she made. Knowing how

She pleasured him, causing her to get into the rhythm that much more; she moved faster, swifter, harder, burying his cock that much further inside of her aching body.

Jax's eyes rolled back into his head, and he cried out her name over and over until reaching sheer ecstasy. The throbbing of his shaft's release caused her body to shake all over with raw pleasure until she reached her little piece of heavenly bliss. After coming back down from their cloud of pure ecstasy, Kaitlyn laid on Jax's chest.

"I love you, Jax, more than anything in this world. I could not imagine anywhere else that I'd rather be in your arms right now," Kaitlyn whispered, kissing his chest.

"I love you more, Kaitlyn. I don't even want to imagine my life without you or our son in it. I only wish that I could give you more. You deserve it all."

"Jax, I have enough. There is nothing more that I want than your love and the love of our boy," Kaitlyn insisted.

Jax smiled sadly at her words, knowing they weren't entirely true; a tear slid from his eye. He knew she wanted to be his wife, and he hated that he could not. He ran his hand through her hair and closed his eyes, trying to fall asleep to her breathing. Kaitlyn knew he was falling asleep; she smiled, letting his heartbeat against her ear soothe her troubled mind. She knew it hurt him that he could not marry her; she hated it herself, but their love was strong and genuinely mattered to her. She closed her eyes, letting herself drift to the world of dreams.

Kaitlyn slept; Bailey's face popped into her mind. She missed her and wished desperately that she could see her again. She tried to find her once when she first had Tristen, but she couldn't. She decided that tomorrow, she would ask Jax to help her look for Bailey once more; she knew in her heart that she had to see her again—she just had to.

3

Bailey woke up early this morning feeling like today would change her life; all night, she dreamed of Kaitlyn as if she had been calling her. She knew it seemed a bit ridiculous, but she didn't care. She just had to believe. She pulled on a pair of her favorite apple-bottom jeans and slid her slinky black tank top over her head down her breasts. She quickly brushed the tangles from her blond hair, slapped on a pair of pumps, and ran from the hotel room. Outside her hotel, she flagged down a taxi, smiled seductively at the driver, handed him some money, and told him where to take her. The moment she reached the club, Bailey was approached by her boss.

"Bailey, the Seeds of Sorrow are putting on a huge concert in San Diego tomorrow night. The band has requested one of the exotic dancers to dance on their stage as they perform, and I was hoping you could do it. You are my best dancer; I know you enjoy their music; you will get in free and have a backstage pass and three thousand dollars. So, Bailey, will you do it?"

It was a sign Bailey knew this; she hated the thought of Kaitlyn finding out she was a stripper. She bit her lower lip and sighed. "All right, I'll do it, but I need money for the costume."

Bailey's boss gave her the night off to prepare for the show and the money to buy a new costume for the show with no argument. "Just make sure you are excellent and very sexy. I need you to put on the show of your life, kid, or you are fired," her boss warned with a wink.

Bailey was nervous yet excited, nervous that Kaitlyn might look down on her and her new lifestyle, excited that she would be performing with one of her favorite and best bands ever while getting to be reunited with her long-lost friend. Suddenly, she thought of Nick; god help her. She would have to face him again just when she finally got over him. She threw her head up, screw him she thought he was nothing.

Later, Bailey caught a taxi to one of her favorite shops in California. She thumbed through all the corsets in Versace, trying to find the perfect one for the show, and finally, she chose a white silk one with antique lace and diamonds sequence on it. She picked it because it reminded her of Kaitlyn and how pure she had been, so she bought it. After purchasing the perfect costume, she flagged down another taxi and headed off to get her hair done. In the beauty salon, Bailey had her long blond hair trimmed and put into tight spiral curls, wanting to look like a sassy Marilyn Monroe. Kaitlyn, my dearest friend, she thought, I can't wait to see you again.

"Bailey honey, what's the occasion? You got a new act at the club or what," her hairdresser asked, snapping her out of her daydream.

"No, I'm performing at a Seeds of Sorrow concert tomorrow night."

Her hairdresser squealed in delight, then began to ramble on and on. "Their lead singer is to die for, the most handsome man I have ever seen. It's a shame he isn't single. Did you know he had a baby boy a little over a year ago with his girlfriend? Strangely, no one knows much about the woman; Jax keeps her identity secretive. It is a publicity stunt; what do you think, Bailey?"

Bailey gasped in shock as she asked, "What did you say, a baby?"

"Yes, why," the hairdresser asked.

Bailey could not believe it; they had a baby together. She was so shocked that she sat there and silently counted back to the baby's birth date, realizing Kaitlyn must have been pregnant when Jax had gone after her at her father's. It was a miracle that Kaitlyn had not lost it; poor thing, she thought she had to have been so terrified. Thinking of this made her want to see her that much more. She tried to hold her and tell her she wished she had been there for her; tomorrow, she whispered to herself, " We shall meet again, my sweet sister.

4

"Jax," Kaitlyn shouted in an irritated tone.

Jax looked up from practicing with the band for tonight's show there in San Diego. He was tired from the long plane ride there from France and was in no mood to argue with Kaitlyn right then, but as he looked into her grey eyes, he knew it was coming. He could see how angry she was by the way she bounced their son in her arms, and it hit him like a ton of bricks. She found out about the stripper they hired for the show. Usually, he would be amused by her jealousy of him, but tonight, he was in no mood to tolerate it.

By the daggers Jax shot in her direction, Kaitlyn could see they would be at war over this particular issue. She could not believe there was going to be some sleazy stripper on stage with the band. She was determined to have her say on whether he liked it. Ignoring him momentarily, she stalked across the room and handed Tristen to Nick.

"Can you guys give me a moment alone with Jax? We need to talk," Kaitlyn asked. Nick and the others looked from Jax back to her and shook their heads, thinking it was going to be a long day, especially after Kaitlyn pissed Jax off. They all walked out of the room, dreading what the rest of the day would bring and that night on and off stage.

When everyone exited the room, Jax grabbed Kaitlyn by the arm and turned her to face him. His eyes searched the depths of her grey ones, which burned with intense anger. "It's just a part of the show, Kaitlyn. The guys and I decided it would get the audience's attention, that's all, and it's going to happen, baby, so there's no point in saying a word to me about it," he hissed through clenched teeth. Tears of frustration threatened to fill Kaitlyn's eyes; she tried to free herself from his iron grip on her arm.

"Damn it, Jax, you know we're not married, I," Kaitlyn was interrupted by his mouth crushing roughly upon hers; at first, this angered her even further until she felt his tongue caress her own, his teeth nibbling the tender flesh of her bottom lip. All angry thoughts seized, and her body instantly responded to him and his passionate kisses. She sighed; it seemed she had lost yet another battle with him. She kissed him back, her hands sliding through his hair, his scent filling her nostrils, making her want to beg him to make love to her.

Jax stopped kissing Kaitlyn, looked deep into her eyes, and grinned. "So baby, how does it feel to be kissed speechless," he teased.

Kaitlyn rolled her eyes and shoved at his chest playfully. He caught her arms, pulling her to the floor, where they landed softly on one another. He tickled at her ribs, making her laughter fill the room. She reached up and caressed his jawline gently with just the tips of her fingers.

"You know what that does to me, my love. Now you will have to face my passion," Jax grinned.

"Oh, please, Jax, punish me," Kaitlyn purred.

Meanwhile, Bailey sat backstage, waiting to meet with the band; as she waited, she looked into the mirror at her reflection to see her hair and makeup. She smiled proudly at her curly blond locks in a twisted bun with tiny ringlets hanging around her dainty face. Her makeup was dark and as sparkly as a star shining in the dead of night, set off by her costume, which showed off every curve of her long, luxurious body. She couldn't wait to see the look on Kaitlyn's face when she saw her again, and she couldn't wait to see the baby. She knew it had to be adorable being the child of Kaitlyn and Jax, and she wondered if it would look like them. Her thoughts were interrupted immediately when she heard the door to her room open.

Bailey turned to see Nick and the other band members staring at her in total shock that she was the stripper for the show that night. Bailey stared back at Nick as a smile curved across his tempting mouth, and her eyes widened. How could she have forgotten how tall and broad-shouldered he was? Lord help her. He was even more handsome than she remembered. His once short brown hair was past his chin almost to his broad shoulders and darkened beautifully. He had a beard where he was once clean-shaven, and his brown eyes now sparkled with desire. Just thinking of how his mouth had felt on her flesh those two years ago made moister gather between her thighs. She hated that he was having this effect on her even now after he had hurt her so deeply in the past.

Nick stood in silence, a grin on his face as he thought of how he never expected to see Legs again. Yet there she was, standing in front of him, looking sexier than ever with her tight lace corset showing off her curves in all the right places. She was stunning from her firm round breasts down to her curvy yet slender thighs. Just the thought of her naked beneath him caused his cock to stiffen in his jeans. "Legs, long time no see, baby," he said in a husky voice.

Nick's voice was so deep and resonant, his accent sheer seduction, yet it did not stop the anger that boiled inside of Bailey. She glared at him, wanting to slap him for calling her baby and Legs; how dare he act like he was someone special to her? Instead of hitting him, she looked him deep in the eyes and said in a haughty tone. "It's Bailey, not Baby or Legs, or did you even know my real name."

Nick laughed at Bailey, thinking she must be playing hard to get. It made him want her a thousand times more, but Jax walked into the room with Kaitlyn and Tristen at his side before he could comment.

"Bailey," Kaitlyn squealed. Bailey walked swiftly over to her, wrapping her free arm around her. She couldn't believe she was there. Then it hit her that Bailey was the exotic dancer for tonight's show. Kaitlyn was speechless, wondering how she had become such a thing. Bailey smiled shyly at her and hugged her back. Unsure what to say, Kaitlyn handed little Tristen to her.

"This is my son, Tristen Jax. He is almost two years old," Kaitlyn smiled. Bailey thought Tristen was the sweetest baby she had ever seen. He was just as handsome as his daddy and lovely as his mommy.

Jax knew Kaitlyn would want to spend some time alone with Bailey, so he motioned for Nick and the others to follow him from the room. As they walked away, Nick whistled at Bailey. "I will see you later, sweetness," he taunted with a wink.

Jax smiled when he saw the apparent sparks between Bailey and Nick. He thought perhaps his friend had finally found his match, just as he had found in Kaitlyn. Maybe it was Nick's turn to fall in love and see why Kaitlyn meant so much to him. Jax asked him what was up with him and Bailey in their hotel room.

"So, man, tell me what is up with how you looked at Bailey just now. Are you still interested in her after all this time?"

"Let's just say that she and I have unfinished business that I intend to take care of as soon as possible," Nick smiled.

Jax shook his head because he could tell by Nick's look that he was more than just attracted to Bailey; he refused to admit it to himself. Meanwhile, she and Kaitlyn were getting caught up in Bailey's dressing room.

"Kaitlyn, what happened those two years ago when Jax went after you and your father? I mean, why did you leave college and me behind? What caused you to do this," Bailey asked.

Kaitlyn knew she shouldn't tell her this, but Bailey was her dearest friend. She had to trust her enough to be honest with her. She motioned for her to sit down, and once she did, Kaitlyn. I began to tell her about the most terrifying night of her life. "I remember waking up in our dorm room to a strange sound, and that was when I saw my father standing over my bed. I remember asking him why he was there, and he started rambling about me being sinful and needing to be punished, saying that it was my judgment day. I struggled with him when he tried to drag me from the bed. He grabbed my hair, slamming my head into the wall; I blacked out. I couldn't be sure what took place. All I knew was that I had woken up in my old bedroom, tied to the bed. Oh, Bailey, it was horrid, especially the things he said and how he beat me. I still have scars on my back from that razor strap of his. He was mad, even tried to rape me. I just wanted to die."

"He what? I can't believe it, his daughter, Kaitlyn. I'm so sorry," Bailey whispered.

"That is another thing, Bailey, he lied. He wasn't my father at all. He found me as a newborn on the steps of his church. I thought I was going to die when his attempts to rape me failed; he tried to strangle me, and he thought he had killed me. I don't remember much after that except Jax coming to me and begging me to wake up, then telling me he had accidentally killed my father."

"Killed, oh my, but the police, they understood, right? That's why you are here with Jax safe, right?"

"We didn't call the police, Bailey. I was pregnant, and Jax was too frightened that if we did, they would lock him up, so we ran. I need you to swear to me right here and now that you will never utter a word of this to anyone," Kaitlyn demanded hoarsely.

Tears were falling down Bailey's face. She walked behind Kaitlyn and raised her shirt to see the scars that still lay across her back from the lashing her father had given her. She was glad Jax accidentally killed that bastard because she knew she would have done the same. Still looking at Kaitlyn's scars, she said she would take their secret to her grave. She sweetly kissed her scars.

"I wish I had been there for you, Kaitlyn, instead of with my parents. After you left, everything went straight to hell. I can't tell you how many times I thought about trying to find you, but I feared that you no longer wanted me in your life. I am so sorry," Bailey cried.

There was a knock at the door before Kaitlyn could reply to Bailey's apology. "Come in," she shouted.

It was Jax and the nanny standing in the doorway. Jax smiled warmly at her as he walked towards the playpen that Tristen lay playing in. He swiftly grabbed him up into his arms and kissed him. Tristen squealed, smiling up at him. Bailey's heart leaped as she saw Jax's love for his son and Kaitlyn; she wished Nick had loved her like that. Her pain grew tenfold as she watched Jax pull Kaitlyn into a soft, passionate kiss.

"Kaitlyn, Bailey, it is show time. Are you two ready?" Jax asked; after ending Kaitlyn and his kiss, he laid Tristen in his nanny's arms.

"I hate to rush you two; I know you two have much catching up to do, but if we don't get a move on it, we will be late getting out on stage."

"It is fine; we can catch up after the show, Bailey." Kaitlyn smiled. Bailey nodded in a silent yes, returning Kaitlyn's sweet smile with one of her own.

"Good. I will be at the corner of the stage, watching you and the rest of the band.

Good luck out there," Kaitlyn winked.

"Thank you, but with you as a friend who needs luck," Bailey shook her head, grinning. Kaitlyn watched with a heavy heart as Jax followed her to the back so they could walk out onto the stage together. She was so glad to have her best friend back in her life.

5

Bailey was about to walk out onto the stage during the band's intro music when she felt someone's strong arms grab her around the waist. She turned to find Nick smiling at her wickedly, making her heart pound at the speed of a lightning bolt. She sighed as he pulled her against his chest and whispered in her ear. "You look incredibly sexy tonight, and I can't wait to watch you dance on that stage." His lips barely brushed the flesh of her ear, sending shivers down her spine.

Bailey's reaction to Nick angered her, and she twisted from his embrace, slapping him across the face. Nick smirked at the sting of her slap. It excited him, causing his cock to shift in his pants. He grabbed her harder, pulling her back to him, lowering his lips from her ear; he gently brushed them against hers. Bailey knew she should stop Nick, but his kiss felt so good, causing her body to ache for more; she trembled all over, from her lips to her legs. A shaky sigh escaped her, and she could not deny the attraction that pulled so strongly between them. She knew she must fight it unless she wished him to crush her spirit as he did her heart in the past. The sound of all the fans shouting for the band broke the trance she was in; shoving Nick from her, she ran out onto the stage, thinking she had to get away from him before he broke down all the walls she built around her heart.

Jax started singing; Bailey ran up to the pole on the stage next to him, twirling and twisting, shaking her body. She danced for Nick tonight to show him what he would never have again. She knew she had the prance, had what he wanted, and intended to use it to taunt him. She was going to get her revenge one way or the other for how he treated her three years ago, and she intended to use all her anger and thirst for vengeance to stop the unwanted desire she felt for him tonight.

Nick watched Bailey's body move to the beat of the music, twisting and shaking all over that damned pole. His desire to touch her naked flesh caused his shaft to burn as hot as the fires of hell. He swore he was going to get her in his bed if it killed him and that, in the end, he would have her screaming his name and begging him for more. He watched her becoming bewitched by her beauty, dark lashes, and high cheekbones that set off her eyes beautifully. His eyes roamed further to her sensual mouth. Her lips were full, and she begged for a man's kisses. She was perfect; her skin was smooth, and her body was lush and full of just the right curves. That blonde hair that shone like pale gold; how he ached to have her trembling in his arms.

Kaitlyn watched from the edge of the stage as Bailey continued to dance, noticing how her eyes frequently looked towards Nick. It was evident that she was dancing for him. Kaitlyn's eyes glanced at Nick to see he, too, was staring at Bailey in return. This was a bit confusing because she thought that Bailey had told her she had no interest in him anymore, yet she was performing her dance as if it were for his eyes alone. Not wanting to ponder these thoughts any longer, Kaitlyn looked away, deciding to speak to Bailey about this matter later after the show.

Kaitlyn's eyes left Bailey scanning the stage until they stopped on Jax; even if she had been with this man thousands of times, just looking at him took her breath away. She wondered if that was how Bailey felt when she looked at Nick tonight. She knew when she first met Nick that she hated him, but after getting to know him these past two years, she found that he wasn't all that bad; he was just a bit wild and afraid of commitment. She laughed, thinking it almost seemed he was scared he would grow old if he fell in love. Maybe Bailey could be the woman who changed his stupid views. She thought she could tame the beast inside him as she tamed the wolf in Jax.

Bailey was exhausted from all the dancing she had just done when the concert finished; she was more than ready to take a load off. She could not wait to see Kaitlyn and Tristen again and followed Jax and the others off the stage. She felt little beads of sweat threatening to roll down her face, making her feel like she was boiling in hot water from the lights on the stage. She shook her head, swearing the heat up there had more than likely turned her milky skin bronzed; all these discomforts seemed to fade away when she saw Kaitlyn smiling at her. She was beyond relieved to see no signs of disappointment in those grey eyes of her dearest friend.

"Bailey, you got to teach me to dance like that," Kaitlyn said excitedly. She winked at Bailey and wrapped her arm around her shoulder. Jax heard Kaitlyn's comment and turned to face them with a devilish grin, making it evident that he liked the idea of Bailey teaching Kaitlyn a few moves. Kaitlyn smiled back at Jax, grabbing him by his shirt, and she pulled him into a passionate kiss.

Bailey watched Jax and Kaitlyn embrace, not noticing that Nick quietly came up behind her; he whispered in her ear.

"You were beautiful out there, Bailey, and so very sexy."

Bailey did not have a moment to argue or reply, for Nick brought his hand around her and caressed her breast with his thumb. She was so caught off guard that she sighed out loud, her face flashing crimson, knowing he heard her sigh. She saw red when a devious laugh escaped him. It drove her mad that he knew her body as well as she; she hated how sure he was of himself after all, what made him so damned confident that she would ever let him have his way with her again. She secretly wished that she was as confident as she sounded in her mind, confident that she wouldn't let him seduce her.

When Jax kissed her back, Kaitlyn almost lost all thoughts of Bailey. She tore her gaze away from him to see an annoyed Bailey standing next to Nick. It was apparent that Nick was taunting her. Kaitlyn gently shoved Jax aside and approached her friend. She pulled Bailey to her side, and they walked hand in hand behind the stage.

Jax glanced up at Nick. They smiled; tonight, they had plans for the women they desired. They all reached the room behind the stage, where Kaitlyn turned to Bailey with mischief in her eyes. "So, how about we do a little dance together for Jax and the boys," she asked. Bailey smiled at Kaitlyn; feeling naughty, she shook her head yes.

"Why only dance? Let's give them a little peep show, shall we," Bailey grinned in mischief. Kaitlyn glanced at her, thinking she could not believe she had forgotten how much fun they used to have together. A devious grin crossed her lips, and she shook her head in silent agreement, thinking it would be a great way to get Nick and Bailey together, as well as Jax, all fired up. She swore they had their best lovemaking when he was angry with her. Bailey and Kaitlyn finally reached the hotel room, finding that Nick and Jax were already drinking.

Everywhere Bailey looked, she could see half-naked groupies and other VIP guests mingling with the band. She sighed, remembering her days as a groupie, shocked to discover she missed them. A man offered her a drink, ending her memories. She grabbed up the shot of whiskey he offered and drank it in one gulp. She was shocked when she turned around to find Kaitlyn doing the same. She smiled, and Bailey grabbed her hand, leading her to a table in the center of the room, laughing at the groupies' shocked faces when they hopped onto the top.

Bailey grabbed the microphone beside them on the table; she screamed into it. "Hey everybody, it's time for a real show; turn up that stereo!"

The people in the room roared, shouting hell yes as music filled the room. Nick and Jax turned from having their fifth shot of whiskey to see Bailey and Kaitlyn standing on a table in the middle of the room, dancing for all eyes to see. Nick's eyes widened, thinking it was possibly the sexiest thing he had ever seen. He watched as Bailey ran her hands through Kaitlyn's hair while Kaitlyn danced dirty with her, moving her hands down Bailey's thighs. He could hardly believe his eyes; it was the side of Kaitlyn he had never seen before; his shaft strained tight against his pants when Bailey pulled Kaitlyn into a kiss. The straining turned to a burning ache when Kaitlyn tore Bailey's corset, revealing her perky white breasts.

"Damn," he shouted, burning with intense desire for Bailey's sweet body; he had to have her tonight; he just had to.

Jax was in utter shock to see his Kaitlyn on top of a table making out with Bailey; even if he was burnt with jealousy, he admitted to himself that a part of him was turned on. He already knew just how hot both these women were in bed, and it was that fact alone that kept him from pulling Kaitlyn off of that table and into his bed. Kaitlyn looked at him, and he knew she could tell by the gleam in his emerald eyes that her little dance immensely turned him on. He smiled, proud that she was his and no one would ever take her from him.

Kaitlyn was glad to see the lust and desire in Jax's eyes; now she had to find a way to get him jealous enough to get her, and she would have it made. Tonight, she wanted the wild beast in him, not the gentle prince, because she wanted him to take her long and hard, not soft and lingering. An idea hit her like lightning, and she asked Bailey to rip her dress slightly. "Bailey, rip my dress just a little, enough to show a tiny bit of skin, and I will do the same to yours," she whispered in her friend's ear.

Bailey knew exactly what Kaitlyn was up to that she wanted Jax to be fired up with rage so he'd drag her off the table and have his way with her. She laughed, loving this wild, not-so-innocent side of her friend. In one solid movement, Bailey tore Kaitlyn's dress down the middle, letting Kaitlyn's voluptuous breasts spring forth; for kicks, she lowered her lips to them and licked one of her nipples. Kaitlyn was caught off guard when Bailey licked her, and she squealed in shock. Looking up quickly afterward to see a fire in Jax's eyes, she knew perhaps Bailey had gone too far.

Jax burned with rage when he saw Kaitlyn's breasts bared for all to see, and in two solid, long strides, he was at the table, throwing her over his shoulders. He walked with her out onto the balcony.

"Jax Alan, put me down now," Kaitlyn screamed.

Jax did as Kaitlyn asked, flinging her down to the balcony floor. He leaned over her with a look of murder in his eyes. She smiled up at him, hoping it would calm the storm within him. Looking into his eyes, she thought he was sexy when he was mad. She pulled her dress bottom up to her waist, baring her satin panties to his stormy eyes. Jax realized instantly that she deliberately made him angry in hopes that he would punish her with his savage passion. Damn, he thought he sure loved this woman; with a devilish grin, he undid the button of his pants, pulling his shaft out for her to see how hard she made him. Kaitlyn moaned in raw desire when he swiftly grabbed her by the legs, pulling her down to him, where he now sat on his knees.

Jax's arousal hardened; he slipped his hand between Kaitlyn's legs, making her gasp, gripping her small hands onto his shoulder. She was already wet and hot with desire. It amazed him how merely touching her like this brought him to such a state of arousal that he felt he would burst inside and out. He knew what she liked, what she wanted, and what would drive her mad with want. He stroked the heated flesh between her thighs in a slow, seductive manner. He continued to stroke her with one hand as the other finished undoing the fly of his jeans, releasing his hardened shaft further.

Kaitlyn whimpered and then wrapped her legs around his muscular thighs. Jax guided his cock into her, thrusting deep, roughly into her soft, slick heat. She sucked in a hard breath, and he felt her tighten around him as they soared into a blaze of everlasting pleasure.

Back inside the hotel room, Bailey was dancing with another member of the band, Shane. She wanted to burn Nick as he burnt her two years ago, so she shook and rubbed her body all over Shane, all the while she kept her eyes on Nick. She knew he was jealous and loved it because she would get at least a small amount of revenge on him tonight. Nick was boiling inside as he continued to watch Legs with Shane, shit he thought, her name is Bailey, not Legs. He could hardly stand to see her rubbing all over him, one of his best friends and bandmates. He knew what she was doing to get to him, to make him jealous, and the sad thing was that it was still working.

When Nick saw Bailey kiss Shane, that was the last damn straw. He ran over to her, grabbing her by the arm. She turned to face him, shooting daggers into his brown eyes from her blue ones, causing Shane to realize they had unfinished business, so he walked away. Bailey swung at Nick with her free hand, trying to slap him, but he caught her hand, pinning it behind her back. He also tightened his grip on her other hand so she could not get away from him. Bailey cursed and then tried to spit in his face; he backed her up against the wall, pushed his head against hers, and through clenched teeth, he spoke. "If you want to play rough, I'll be more than happy to oblige; however, I'd prefer to be gentle with you."

A breathless Bailey sighed. "It's too late, Nick. It's too late for us; leave me alone. You lost any chance with me a long time ago. I am too tired to fight with you any longer tonight. Just let me go," she begged.

Nick could see so many emotions in Bailey's beautiful blue eyes, but the one that stood out was stabbed at his heart. It was pain, so much pain, and what bothered him the most was to know he had caused all of it. He raised his hand, caressing her cheek. "Is there nothing I can do to change your mind, Bailey? I was thinking about whether you were lonely. Maybe we could listen; it's not like me to say I'm sorry," Nick stopped talking. He pulled Bailey closer and kissed her, raising his left hand to caress her face again. He broke the kiss only a moment later to finish speaking. He raised his eyes to hers.

"Bailey, I've missed you more than you could ever imagine," his voice became breathless.

"I know you've missed me too; I want you," he murmured, kissing the corners of her lips again. Bailey's body trembled from the soft kiss Nick bestowed upon her. She moaned softly, opening her mouth to kiss him back; the feeling of his warm tongue caressing her own sent a bolt of raw desire all through her. Her mind screamed, kissed, loved, and never let me go. Nick's lips left hers to trail along the line of her jaw. Her head dropped back instinctively, and he kissed the hollow of her throat. She felt her knees growing weak; his hand slid from her face to her breasts, where he caressed her taunt nipples. She was suddenly returned to reality when he whispered in her ear again.

"I remember the last time we made love like it was only yesterday."

These words Nick whispered reminded Bailey how he left her behind, never looking back, and she shoved him from her body. "Don't you touch me again because I remember how you left me without saying goodbye? How you treated me like I was nothing but your whore," she yelled?

Nick stared at Bailey in silence for a long time until he lost his temper and said something stupid. "You knew damn well there was nothing real going on between us then. If you didn't like it, you knew where that door was." He regretted these words when he saw tears roll from Bailey's eyes. He stepped closer to her, trying to touch her, and she kneed him right between the legs. Nick bit into his lip in agony while she hurried away.

Bailey had to get away from Nick before she killed him; she ran out into the middle of the room, grabbed a bottle of whiskey, and emptied it in a solid breath. She grabbed Shane by his shirt, pulling him into a fiery kiss. Being trashed, Shane responded to this with an even deeper one. One kiss kept leading to another until they ended up in his bed for the remainder of the night.

Nick sat against the wall, holding his injured pride and manhood in his hands, watching Bailey and Shane go to bed. As he watched, he felt so much rage that it scared him; he needed to get out of there before he went after them and hurt Shane. Jax needed anyone; he knew only he could help him calm down before he did something stupid.

6

Jax lay on the balcony floor with Kaitlyn wrapped tightly in his arms; he stared into the sky, remembering the first time he saw her standing in the front row of a crowd of fans. He remembered how she looked at him directly as if she were reading his mind and soul. He also recalled how he felt whole the second he touched her hand when she fell in the middle of the crowd. He wished Nick and Bailey could find those things in each other. He knew Kaitlyn wouldn't want to lose her friend again. He wanted nothing but happiness for her. After all, he would never be able to give her the one thing she wanted and needed the most.

Kaitlyn lay wrapped in Jax's strong arms, hoping Bailey and Nick would stop fighting their feelings for one another. She wanted Bailey to find the love and joy she found with Jax. As if reading each other's thoughts, Jax and Kaitlyn turned in each other's arms.

"Jax, do you think there is any hope for Nick and Bailey as a couple," Kaitlyn asked.

"They need one another just as badly as I needed you, my love. I hope they can overcome all their past issues first," he sighed.

"Do you think you could ask Bailey to come along for the rest of the tour," Kaitlyn asked sweetly.

"Anything you want, sweetness," he grinned; their conversation abruptly stopped when they heard a loud crash inside the hotel room.

Jax jumped up from the balcony floor, pulling Kaitlyn up, too. Together, they rushed inside, finding a very tipsy Nick fighting with their drummer, Shane. Nick had thrown him across one of the tables and broken it. He now stood over him, fixing to bash him over the head with an empty whiskey bottle. Jax grabbed Nick by the shirt and flung him across the room, pulling Shane to his feet.

"Are you all right, Shane? Did Nick hurt you," he asked. Shane shook his head, said he was fine and left the room. Soon after, Jax followed Nick's gaze over to the other side of the room to find Bailey lying utterly naked in Shane's bed.

Like Jax, Kaitlyn knew precisely what happened between Nick and Shane; Bailey slept with Shane to hurt Nick for how he hurt her in the past. Kaitlyn's eyes locked with Bailey's, indicating that she was shocked by Nick's reaction to seeing her in Shane's bed.

"Kaitlyn, take Bailey and go check on our son in the other room now," Jax growled. Usually, Kaitlyn wouldn't put up with Jax demanding her like this, but this time, she knew it was wise to do as she was told. She quickly helped Bailey to dress, and then they exited the room.

As Kaitlyn and Bailey exited the room, Jax approached Nick and held out his hand to him. Nick took it, and the two walked over to the table and sat silently for the night. Jax knew this was no time to talk to Nick and that he was far too lost in his thoughts to listen to reason. He knew that if he had walked in on Kaitlyn with another, he would have reacted similarly, if not worse, than with Shane.

Meanwhile, across the room, Kaitlyn sat with Bailey brooding, "What the hell were you thinking, Bailey? Do you have any idea what the problems you just caused were?"

"I... umm, it wasn't supposed to," Bailey couldn't keep her tears at bay any longer. She stopped trying to explain herself, letting them fall like a river from her eyes. She buried her face in her hands like a child's. Kaitlyn's irritation faltered at Bailey's tears. She hugged her tightly, letting her cry until no more tears were left.

When Bailey finally stopped crying, Kaitlyn lifted her arms from around her and smiled at her.

"Bailey, it is obvious that there is still something between you and Nick. Listen, Jax told me he was cool with you coming on the tour with us. Will you?" Kaitlyn begged.

Bailey smiled; she loved being with Kaitlyn and Tristen, even if she dreaded facing Nick and Shane daily after what she had done that night. She bit her lower lip until her love for Kaitlyn prevailed. "I can't imagine anywhere else I would rather be than here with you and Tristen. I have no intention of acting on my old feelings for Nick. I will go with you only because I am not ready to lose you again. I have missed you so much, Kaitlyn, more than you can imagine; you are my only friend."

"Oh Bailey, I'm so glad. We will have loads of fun, and you won't regret it. We can visit all the stores on the coast and shop until we drop. I have been so lonely without you in my life."

"Kaitlyn, I can't wait to do all those things we missed with you, but first, I have to face Nick and what happened with him and Shane. You know what they say: there is no time like the present. I hope Nick has had enough time to calm down." She stood up to go back to where the others were.

Once inside the room with the band, Bailey's fear subsided. She found Nick passed out cold on the floor. Her eyes roamed the room to find that Jax had fallen asleep, too. She glanced back to where Kaitlyn stood and saw she was just as exhausted." I will talk to Nick and Shane later. You look exhausted, Kaitlyn. Maybe you should go to bed. I will be here when you wake up. I am going to take a nap myself," Bailey smiled weakly.

Not wanting any more fighting, Kaitlyn smiled back at her, walked over to Jax, and laid on his chest. Bailey walked alone to Nick's bed, secretly wishing he loved her as Jax loved Kaitlyn. She fell to the mattress, and her thoughts drifted in her mind fast as she fell into a deep sleep.

"Nick, Nick," Bailey whimpered.

Nick woke up to the sound of his name being called repeatedly. He looked over to his bed to see Bailey asleep, her lips parting slightly as she whimpered his name repeatedly as if he were making love to her. A smile curved across his mouth as he thought Shane must not have been what she needed, that it was obvious since she was dreaming of him instead. She was calling his name as if they were making passionate love. He walked over to the bed and leaned over her sleeping body, swearing she was the most beautiful woman he had ever seen, especially when she was like this. She looked so peaceful and angelic, her blond curls hanging down her face and her lips parted to reveal her pearly white teeth. He wanted to kiss her lips and taste the sweetness of her skin in his mouth. He ran his thumb across her bottom lip, causing her to smile as she continued to sleep. Her smile sent tingles all through his body, making him want her so bad he thought he might go insane.

Bailey wakes up to find Nick leaning over her, looking at her like he owns her. She sits up so fast she nearly bumps heads with him. She glares at him for startling her, wanting badly to scold him, but seeing the devilish grin on his handsome face, she cannot speak.

"What's wrong, Bailey? Shane wasn't brave enough for you? Did you need to dream of me, and how can only I please you?' Nick teased in a husky voice that sent shivers all down Bailey's spine. She could feel the heat rise to her cheeks when she recalled the dream she was having before he woke her up. She was ashamed, realizing she must have cried his name out loud that he had heard her. She was so embarrassed that all she could do was scold him for his behavior toward her and Shane for hooking up.

"What's it to you anyhow? Why did you act like such an ass last night when I slept with Shane?" Bailey's words angered Nick, and she saw the proof in his eyes when he leaned in to answer her. She trembled when he pulled her against him; instead of yelling at her, he looked deep into her eyes, making her extremely uncomfortable.

"I care because I want you for myself and don't want anyone else touching you. I tried to break his neck for touching you. I wanted to put his eyes out for looking at you. I want to hear you call my name as you do when you're sleeping, and here you are, running scared. Stop and let me take you like only I can take you," he demanded. Bailey was ready to refuse when he pressed his lips to hers and kissed her deeply.

His unexpected kiss caused the passion that simmered between them to erupt.

Nick could feel Bailey's heart pounding in her breasts as his lips and tongue tasted of hers. He knew she wanted him and was determined to prove it to her. He slid his hand into her dress and caressed her tender breasts. Her skin felt so soft, like silk, tempting him until he wanted to taste it. Her nipples became hard beneath the caress of his fingers. She moaned against his lips. His left hers to trail down to her ear, where he nibbled and whispered words of passion.

"Let me remind you how well we fit together and burn in each other's embrace."

Bailey knew she should stop Nick, but his hands and mouth were such a sweet torcher to her body that she could barely resist giving herself to him. He kissed her neck until she could feel the warm wetness of his tongue tasting her, sending her senses reeling. Her body was growing limp as she struggled to control the desire he brought out in her. She could feel his hand sliding up her skirt between her thighs. She became so lost in the moment that she let him caress her as he had years ago.

"Just let me touch you here, Bailey; I want to feel the wetness of your body," Nick whispered, slowly sliding his hands up her inner thigh to the patch of blond curls between them. There, his long fingers spread across her quivering body, teasing and taunting her. She was so slick and hot that when he lowered his mouth, nibbling at her neck once more, anticipation gripped her. She wanted his fingers, his mouth, his cock, and she could not bite back her sigh of complete surrender.

Nick heard Bailey's sigh, and he pushed his fingers inside of her as if he heard her wicked thoughts, her legs spread wider. She clung to him, crying out in pleasure from the entry of his fingers into her neither region. She almost forgot how good they felt when he used them to give her pleasure; her body burned with desire. She began to shake all over, laying back on the bed, letting this desire take control of her body and thoughts. Nick's fingers worked their magic, withdrawing and then entering her heated core over and over again until her body exploded with raw pleasure.

Bailey arched her hips up slightly, and Nick's hands slid to grip her thighs; leaning forward, he replaced his fingers with his mouth. She sucked in a hard breath whimpering as the tension inside her grew. He tightened his hold on her, sending her spiraling toward sweet release. She wanted him to take her now, end this sweet torment. She twined her fingers in his shoulder-length hair, pulling his mouth back to hers. Her tongue met and mated with his as their need bonded them together. She felt his hot breath mingling with her own and heard his heated groan. It made her desire burn hotter than the flames of hell.

Bailey's naked flesh felt absurdly enticing, her skin smooth and warm. She was beautiful, angelic, and dangerously seductive. Nick's shaft throbbed with the desire to touch the inside of her tight, hot sheath. He quickly unbuttoned his pants, letting his long stiff shaft spring forth; taking it in his hand, he rubbed the tip over her passionate swollen nether lips and clit. She cried out his name and thrust her hips up for him to take her. With a growl, he slammed his cock deep inside of her, desperate to brand her his.

Bailey was shivering; every nerve in her body hummed, her blood boiled, and her bones seemed to melt under Nick's savage, animalistic lovemaking. She was sent into eternal bliss at the entry of his long, thick shaft into her all-too-eager body. She ran her hands through his shoulder-length brown hair and begged him for more. She wrapped her legs around him tightly, dragging her nails down his back, causing him to moan in sweet, splendid pleasure. He rolled over, pulling her on top of him, his shaft remaining deep inside of her. She smiled, seeing his eyes roll back in his head when she thrust her hips back and forth, giving him intense pleasure.

"I swear if I live to be a thousand years, nothing will ever feel as good as your succulent body," Nick whispered.

Bailey continued to thrust her hips in perfect accord with Nick until each of the breaths they took turned into pants. No longer able to control the pressure that built deep inside of him, Nick's shaft exploded in sheer ecstasy, filling Bailey with his warm seed. She wilted against him, reaching her delightful bliss. Their physical joining could not have touched her more deeply. Nick slipped as quickly back into her heart and soul as he had her bed. She hated that she had no will or desire to resist him. He rolled her from him and pulled her back against him, holding her in his strong arms, and she lay there quietly in his embrace.

Tears falling from her eyes. Bailey hated herself for letting Nick seduce her so quickly, and she hated him even more for always taking so much from her every time he touched her. She turned in his arms, pushing him from her, pulling her dress back down to cover her naked body. She quickly jumped from the bed, trying to walk away.

Nick jumped from the bed, pulled up his pants, and ran after Bailey. He refused to let her freeze up on him after they made love. He grabbed her arm, spinning her around to face him, and the look in her eyes sent a stab of pain and guilt shooting from his soul to his heart. She had tears running down her face, and her eyes were full of pain.

"Nick, please let me go, leave me alone. I don't want your pity. I have never been loved by a single man who's touched me. Yes, at one time, I cared so much, too much for you. I am no longer that naïve young woman. Truth is, I know that you will never love me, not like I love you," she screamed.

Nick was shocked to hear Bailey's confession to him; he let go of her arm in stunned silence. He knew he should have stopped her, but he was frozen like ice as she turned and walked away. "Nick, go after her; you know you love her more than you let on," he heard Jax say behind him. He turned to see the deep concern in his friend's eyes.

"She's the woman who can drag you down yet pull you up again. Seize the moment, my friend, before you lose her for good. Don't just sit there and let this chance at happiness pass you by. Besides, she's going on tour with us, so you need to get along," Jax insisted.

Nick listened to Jax till he finished, then watched as he walked back over to his bed, where Kaitlyn was still fast asleep. He gently shook her awake. Nick knew Jax was right in his words, he did care for Bailey, and it scared the hell out of him. He had been a loner his entire life and wasn't sure if he wanted that to change. He considered himself a man who called anywhere he laid his head on his home, but the problem was he didn't want her to leave him. He needed Bailey around; he just wasn't sure he could offer her more than what he already had. Feeling frustrated he began to help the band get ready to move on out on the road once more.

Bailey nearly bumped into Jax, Kaitlyn, and Tristen as she ran from the room. Jax caught her when she stumbled back, almost falling. "Are you alright Bailey, you still coming with us," he asked in concern. She looked over at Kaitlyn and Tristen, the look of pleading in Kaitlyn's eyes tore at her heart, she couldn't possibly abandon them.

"I am peachy keen. I will be going, just need a few moments to get my thoughts clear," Bailey lied. Jax let go of her arm, exchanged glances with Kaitlyn then kissed her, reaching for little Tristen, he took him from her arms to leave her and Bailey alone to talk.

"Alright he is gone, now tell me the truth. Are you honestly alright," Kaitlyn asked, her voice thick with concern.

"I think, I mean no, I'm not ok. I let him make love to me again, Kaitlyn, after the way he hurt me in the past. I feel so damned foolish and weak that I even told him I loved him when I know he will never love me back. I never truly got over him. I more than likely never will, so what am I to do now?"

"Nick returns your feelings, Bailey; he is merely afraid of losing his freedom. He is terrified that if he loves you, it will age him. Bailey knew Kaitlyn meant well, but she just could not believe her; happy endings weren't a reality for women like her.

9

Jax, Nick, and the rest of the band sat on the tour bus, waiting for Bailey and Kaitlyn to come aboard. Nick had baby Tristen on his knee, bouncing him, making him laugh and coo. He loved playing with Tristen because he was so cute, and when he laughed, he was like a mini, less anxious version of Jax. It was weird thinking of Jax as a father, but he was a damn good one. He always was available for Tristen and played with him every chance he got. He was also very affectionate with him, kissing and hugging him constantly. It made Nick wonder if he would also be a good father like his friend one day.

Jax watched Nick playing with his son, and he knew he would make a great father one day when he was ready. He hoped when that day arrived, Bailey would be the child's mother because it was apparent that he loved her. Jax lost these thoughts when he heard her, and Kaitlyn finally step onto the bus; he smiled as he watched them walk over to where he now stood. Kaitlyn reached up, kissing him on the cheek. Bailey just smiled and sat on a bed, letting her gaze go to where Nick held Tristen.

Bailey watched Nick playing with Tristen, and she smiled once again. She thought he had a way with children. She could tell by the way his eyes glowed when Tristen smiled or cooed at him that he loved kids. She blushed as he felt her eyes on him, and now looked at her with a sexy smile that made her body tremble. She turned crimson further when she felt the moister gathering slightly between her thighs. Her body began to yearn for his, she wanted to turn her eyes from his heated gaze, but she couldn't muster the strength to move.

Nick knew what Bailey was thinking the second he looked into her eyes, so he stood with Tristen in his arms and walked over to her. He handed Tristen to Kaitlyn, who stood nearby and then held out his hand to Bailey, wanting her to talk with him. The frightened look in her eyes told him that she desperately wanted to refuse, but he was grateful when she did just the opposite, reaching her hand out towards his. "Bailey, I have so much to say to you. I wish I could take back all I took from you. The truth is you make me feel like I really can be a better man. When I touch you, I can hardly breathe. You make me want to scream because your body is like heaven to me. I am scared to feel for you as I do. Just please don't rush this between us; I only need time to think," he begged.

Bailey stood there silently for the longest time before finally walking up to Nick. She threw her arms around his neck; her eyes searched the depths of his. She leaned in for a soft yet passionate kiss. Just the touch of his lips against hers caused her body to ache with intense need. Her skin tingled, her senses reeled, and her heartbeat so rapid she thought it would jump from her chest. His lips and tongue branded her as if they were a hot rod of iron. She realized now that she needed this man, no matter if all he caused her was pain.

Nick was set ablaze by Bailey's passionate kiss. His shaft hardened in his pants, causing them to strain uncomfortably against them. He groaned, lifting her to the dresser in the back of his

Room on the bus. He slid his hands up her dress, causing her thighs to tremble, tearing her silk panties to expose her nether region to the touch of his warm, eager hands. He bent down to kiss her, sliding his fingers between her now parted welcoming thighs to caress her moist heat. She felt so hot, so slick with desire. Her breathing became ragged. His dark eyes smoldered with heat; his jaw clenched tight. His breathing was unsteady, the feel of her driving him to blazing heights of passion. He continued to caress her velvet-like moister, taking her with him on a spiraled road to sheer ecstasy.

Bailey rolled her head back, letting Nick's persistent caresses in her most secret region take her to eternal abandonment. She also rolled her eyes back, feeling his mouth lower to her tender breasts where he used his teeth to pull her top down, exposing them for his view. He nibbled at her now taunt nipples, sending shock waves of delight all through her heated body. She was consumed by him, craving his fingers, his thick shaft more than anything she ever wanted in her entire life.

Nick could tell by the way Bailey squealed and screamed that she needed his fingers and his shaft inside of her succulent body to cool the burning desire he stirred deep inside of her. He bit down on her nipple and thrust his fingers into her tight, warm core. Bailey cried out his name; he silenced her other passionate spoken words, crushing his mouth savagely down upon hers. It

was a mating of the mouths, teeth, and tongue that stole her breath. Air surged from her lungs, and fire replaced it with his tongue. Nick entered and then withdrew inside her warm mouth as his fingers did the same with her womanly core.

Bailey's body convulsed with intense eroticism as she trembled uncontrollably all over. He refused to let her off that easily and vowed by the time he was done, she'd be ruined for any other man. He wanted her to crave him and only him for the rest of her life. He lowered his head between her thighs, wrapping his hands around her legs. He kissed the inside of her thigh, causing her to shake uncontrollably in his hands. He kissed her bud of desire, letting his tongue flick slowly back and forth, tasting the sweetness of dripping honey.

Bailey swore she was going to explode from the intense pleasure Nick's mouth and tongue now gave her body. She ran her hands through his hair. "Nick, please take me now and end this sweet torcher on my body and heart," Bailey begged repeatedly. Each time she begged, he would increase his tongue caress, causing her body to convulse, showering him with her sweet juices all over again.

Finally, Nick stood up from Bailey, unbuttoning his pants; he released his rock-hard shaft, pulling her down from the dresser. He took her hand, placing it on his bulging erection, and she knelt on her knees and kissed the tip of it. His cock throbbed wildly in her warm, soft hands. She smiled up at him and brushed her tongue lightly over the full length of him.

"Bailey," Nick whispered hoarsely, proving how he loved the pleasure she was giving him. Bailey began to suckle at his long, stiff, pulsing shaft until she heard him growl between clenched teeth for her to stand up. She did as he asked, wanting desperately to feel him inside her. She watched as he removed his clothing one piece at a time, her eyes devoured his muscled perfection. He seemed larger now, unclothed. The planes of his chest were well-defined, with nothing but solid muscle.

Nick lifted Bailey yet again to his waist so she could wrap her legs around him, and when they were wrapped tightly in place, he backed her against the wall, thrusting his desire-filled erection wildly into her succulent-seeking body over and over again until she thought she would pass out from the built-up pressure that now burst free from her body.

"Oh God, Nick, make me yours forever, take me like this always," Bailey begged hoarsely.

Her words of passion sent him into a fit of lust and pleasure, and he, in return, called out her name, vowing that he loved her and always would.

Finally, feeling completely spent, Nick slid to the floor taking her with him, he lay on Bailey's breasts, letting her hold him as she ran her fingers through his hair. Being with her like this gave him so much peace, complete and utter endless peace.

Bailey lay wrapped in Nick's arms; she pressed her hand against his cheek. He took her hand and kissed her palm; she thought her heart would stop. She could not imagine loving another the way she loved him, no matter how he had scarred her heart. She knew at that moment that she would love him always. She could not bear to be separated from him ever again.

10

CORA, AKA JEWEL, SAT at the bar of her favorite dance club here in San Diego. Last night, she saw something that made her blood boil: Legs up on stage at a Seeds of Sorrow concert with Jax, Nick, and the rest of the band. It was two years ago when she last saw the slut, and she still hated her and blamed her for everything that happened between her and Jax when she lost him to Kaitlyn. Bailey came to the concert that night to get him to go after Kaitlyn, and he took off without saying a single word to her. The next day, he showed up with Kaitlyn at his side, telling her to get lost, that he never loved her, and that Kaitlyn was the only woman for him. She swore she would never forget how humiliated she had been when Jax dismissed her like trash after she gave him everything she had. He treated her like a common trollop when she had always treated him like he was her very reason for living.

Jewel ordered another shot of her favorite whiskey, stood up from the bar, and walked onto the busy dance floor. She thought perhaps she could get over her burning desire for revenge if she danced. She swung her hips from side to side as man after man came up to her for a dance. The old Jewel would have loved the attention, but now all she saw was Jax, the fact that he discarded her like a used piece of trash. How he had cost her so much, more than he would ever know. She clenched her teeth, deciding she would have that revenge after all. She would have it no matter how she had to go about getting it, no matter who paid the price in the end. If she were destined to be alone for the rest of her life, she would make sure Bailey was, too.

It hit her: the ultimate revenge against Bailey. Cora saw the apparent sparks between her and Nick at last night's show, and she thought she would use him to hurt Bailey. She would break her heart like Jax had broken hers. She knew when she succeeded, it would taste bittersweet. Yes, she thought it was about time she showed Bailey and Kaitlyn what she was made of. She was the worst thing Jax could have done; because of his rejection, she had become maneater-tangled up in revenge and despair, like a poison that spread from person to person. She would rage a war that consumed them all.

Jewel grabbed her dance partner by his shoulders, swinging her body up and down the length of his muscular body. The thought of getting her sweet revenge made her as hot as the fires of hell. She turned and rubbed her firm round bottom against her partner's cock, making it hardened in his tight jeans, thinking tonight she would use this looser to calm her hot, wanton body. She will buy her ticket tomorrow and attend the following Seeds of Sorrow concert. After all, she thought, once a woman resolves to be wicked.... she must be prepared to go all the way.

11

Jewel woke the next day in bed with her dance partner from the night before. She hadn't the faintest idea of his name, which was fine. All that mattered to her was that he was still passed out with his wallet full of money. She slipped from the bed, grabbed the wallet off the floor, took all the money, and left the room, never turning once to think about the man she left with nothing. He was just a toy to play with and pass the time to her. She could have sex with hundreds of men, maybe more, and it would still be the only one face she saw when they were inside of her, Jax. As much as she wanted to hate him, she could not deny she missed him. She missed the way he fucked her. The way his skin and cum tasted on her lips. He was the death of peace and life for her.

After Cora-Jewel purchased her ticket and a VIP backstage pass, she boarded her flight to Atlanta, where the Seeds of Sorrow concert would take place. She laughed out loud, thinking of how shocked Jax would be to see her; at the thought, she could hardly wait to see this reaction. She planned to give them all a show they would never forget. She purchased a skintight mini-dress that was made of pure lace, planning to wear it for the little dance she planned for them all,

Especially Nick. Jewel knew no red-blooded man could resist a hot-blooded woman like herself. She figured Jax had to get bored with Kaitlyn by now, even if she had a child with him. If not, that would be his loss; it does not matter as long as she seduced Nick and destroyed Bailey. All she wanted was for her to feel the same agonizing despair when Jax threw her away for Kaitlyn. Nothing stung her foolish pride more than what he had done all those three years ago, and she wanted in the end, for Bailey was as bitter and alone as she was now and seemed destined to remain until the end of her days.

Jewel's mind became heavy as she kept thinking of her life and how it could have been with Jax if Bailey had left well enough alone. She knew he would have never loved her the way he did Kaitlyn, yet she would have made him a good wife. Before that night, she began to make real progress with him, and he finally stopped calling Kaitlyn's name in his sleep and when they made love. Did Bailey not see she would never get over him, even knowing he could have never truly felt half as much for her as she did for him? Did she not care that taking him away from her would drive her over the edge? It would be a constant reminder that she was never worthy enough in his eyes, becoming her undoing.

Jewel fought back the tears that threatened to fill her eyes as she remembered how bad it hurt her to know she would have never compared to Kaitlyn. She bit back these bitter tears, also thinking of her and Jax's love child that she had given up for adoption, the child he must never know about. A beautiful baby girl with her father's strawberry blonde hair and her mother's green eyes. A delicate creature that she was forced to give up because she was far too full of bitterness and despair to give her the life she deserved. The good sisters of the convent she left her at gave their word she would be cherished.

Suddenly, Jewel's pain again returned to anger; she knew revenge was the only thing she had left now, the only way to free herself of humiliation and despair.

12

THE PAST THREE WEEKS were remarkably interesting for Bailey. She was playing with baby Tristen if she wasn't talking to her dearest friend, Kaitlyn. She was in Nick's bed with him this morning, locked in his strong embrace. Her feelings for him in the past were nothing compared to how she felt about him now. Just the slightest touch of his hand spun her into another world where her desires burned deep within her heart and soul. The touch of his lips on hers made her turn to quicksilver in his embrace. She became his for all eternity, no matter how much pain he may cause her in the end. Each time he made love to her, he branded her very soul, and she became lost to him constantly.

Nick sat on his bed, drinking from his bottle of whiskey and thinking about the past three weeks. No woman ever made him feel the way Bailey did now. He usually just had his way with them and never looked back, but with her, it was like he couldn't get enough. He had never before let a woman in the way he did her, and it scared him. Looking into her crystal blue eyes made his heart pound in his chest. Her kisses and caresses felt so right, like she was put on this earth to be his, and he was to be hers. All these feelings were so unexpected to him, so feared that he wanted just to run, push her away, yet his body always refused to listen to his head.

Kaitlyn sat across from Bailey with her son in her arms and a smile on her face. She was so happy for Bailey, noticing how close she and Nick had become over these three weeks. They were almost as bad as she and Jax, making love wherever and whenever they pleased. Like the two, they cared not who saw or heard them. She loved the look Bailey had in her eyes lately; she hoped Nick wouldn't mess it all up when they got to Atlanta. She knew there were so many temptations for them to have to overcome. Over the past two years, she traveled with the band, and she saw Nick with tons of women doing drugs and other not-so-decent things. Sure, Jax drank a lot and sometimes did a little worse, but he never touched another woman other than her, not since she came to California with him two years ago.

Jax leaned against the wall, gazing across the room at Nick. By the way, he looked at Bailey, he knew he was falling in love with her. The problem was Nick was not looking for love, and it was clear that he was scared as hell. Jax knew he would do everything he could to push Bailey away; he just hoped that she would be strong enough to push back, let him let go of his fears, and give all of himself to her.

Nick looked up to find Jax looking at him with concern. He wished he could talk to him about his fears, his doubts. The problem was he was just too damn proud to admit that he loved Bailey, especially since he always gave him a hard time about Kaitlyn. He smiled at Jax, finished his whiskey, threw the bottle to the floor, and jumped onto his feet, walking away. He had to get away from him and his damn concern-filled eyes before he gave in to his feelings.

Bailey glanced up to see Nick storming from the bus and then looked at Kaitlyn and Tristen. "I will be back in a few, Kaitlyn. I have to see what is going on with Nick," she smiled weakly. Kaitlyn nodded her head in understanding. Bailey kissed Tristen's head and walked towards the bus door.

As Bailey looked out the door, she saw Nick slamming his fists into the bus. She bit her lip and walked closer, wishing she understood what could have made him outraged. "Nick," she said in a shaky tone as she stepped from the bus steps.

Nick looked up to see confusion shining through Bailey's beautiful blue eyes. He wanted to tell her to go back inside the bus, but just looking at her made his heart bleed. He grabbed her hand, pulling her into a rough kiss, and before she could react, he flipped her around, crushing her back against the bus. He tried to slide his hand up her dress; she pushed at his chest. "Nick, stop this, not now, not here; what the hell is wrong with you?" she snarled.

"I am fine. I have a lot of shit on my mind, woman. Is that all right?" Again, Nick kissed Bailey and tried to slide his hand up her dress again.

"Damn it, I said no," Bailey shouted at him. She knew he was lying and angrily walked back onto the bus. In her heart, she knew he was trying to push her away, and it hurt so bad she wanted to hit him, to scream and shout at him. She ached to call him a coward for running from his feelings for her. She flew through the bus back to his bed to get her stuff and stay at the other end.

Nick stormed onto the bus after Bailey. Jax stood in front of him. "Back off, Nick, leave Bailey alone for a while; you've done enough," he hissed. Nick could tell by the look in Jax's eyes that he wasn't asking him; he was telling him to leave her alone. He shook his head, walked over to Kaitlyn, picked Tristen up, and started to play with him.

Jax again looked from Nick to Kaitlyn, silently letting her know he needed to be alone with his friend. Kaitlyn went to the far end of the bus, where Bailey was sitting on Nick's bed crying. She wrapped her arms lovingly around her to hold her tightly. She could just kill Nick for being such a stubborn fool idiot. He didn't deserve her if he didn't realize what a good woman Bailey was. She wanted desperately to walk over to him and slap him so hard that his ears rang for the rest of his pathetic life.

Bailey let all her pain out as Kaitlyn held her, thinking, why couldn't Nick love her the way she loved him, the way she had always loved him? Why couldn't they be more like Kaitlyn and

Jax and accept their feelings? Her heart screamed for his, and he refused to listen. She had no idea how to make him see what he meant to her. She wanted him to stop fighting his love and embrace it as she had.

After Jax lectures him on how he is about to lose the best thing that could have ever happened to him, Nick decides to try to work things out with Bailey. Deep inside, he knew his friend was right, so he handed him his now sleeping son and walked to where Kaitlyn and Bailey stood in silence. By the time he reached them, they were sitting on his bed, talking about how hard it was to live in Jax and his world.

"Kaitlyn, can you give me some time alone with Bailey, please," Nick asked. Kaitlyn reluctantly did as Nick asked, shooting daggers at him; she swore if he didn't watch it, she was going to kick his ass.

Bailey looked at Nick for a moment. She tried to walk away, but he stepped before her, blocking her path to freedom. She let all her pain and frustrations out by slapping him over and over again. Having enough, Nick grabbed her wrist and embraced her tightly. She let him hold her for what seemed like an eternity until he pulled her head up to give her a soft kiss. His kiss burned deep inside of her, bursting her into flames. Her knees grew weak, and moister gathered between her trembling thighs. Damn, this man and the way he made her bend to his will.

Tears slid down her face as he kissed her neck, sliding his hands behind her to caress her firm bottom. She whimpered as his lips went down to her breasts, where he nibbled at her taunt nipples, causing them to strain against her shirt. His warm, strong hands slid her skirt up above her thighs, sliding her lace panties down past her knees.

Nick started at Bailey's knees, kissing them. Tonight, he wanted to kiss and taste her entire body. His way of showing her how much he loved her without having to say words. He felt her legs trembling. He reached the inside of her thighs, brushing feather-like kisses until she squealed in delight. He kissed and caressed her warm, slick heat with his lips and tongue; Bailey ran her shaking hands through his hair, crying out in pleasure. He sucked in a wild breath when her body showered him with its honeyed moister. She began to shake even more as he stood up, pulling her top down to suckle on her nipples.

"Nick, make love to me," she begged. Nick lifted Bailey into his arms and wrapped her legs around him, carrying her to his bed, where he laid her on the soft mattress. She watched him as he took off his shirt.

Nick's upper body was so strong and muscular, like an ancient warrior, and Bailey's gaze slid down his treasure trail to watch him unbutton his pants and then slide them to the floor. His long, thick shaft sprang forth from between his muscled thighs. Bailey felt so hot with passion that she swore she would burst into flames. She spread her thighs for him, and he grabbed her feet, pulling her gently down the bed. He climbed between her parted thighs. "Open for me," he whispered, pressing kisses to her throat, then each breast, on the sensitive skin of her navel.

Nick grasped Bailey's hands, taking her lips with his once more, nipping at them. He smiled wickedly at her, "I love you," he said in a low growl, driving his rock-hard cock deep inside her tight body.

Bailey felt so hot and so tight he thought he would burst; Nick clenched his teeth and thrust harder, deeper into her welcoming sheath. He cried out her name as the pressure built uncontrollably inside of his throbbing male member. Her fingers slid across the bare flesh of his back, and he thrust deeper. Her body convulsed. "I love you more than anything in this world," he whispered. She lifted her hips franticly to meet him, thrust for thrust, shaking from head to toe with raw pleasure, the pressure bursting free from her body like a hurricane.

"Nick, I love you. I need you to breathe, take me, make me yours," Bailey cried out as she reached total abandonment. The feel of her warm, wet body tightening around his shaft caused him to reach total bliss as he shot his warm seed deep into her womanly core.

"Bailey, I love you, I love you, "Nick repeated hoarsely, pulling her tightly into his arms, letting his still throbbing shaft slide from her body.

Bailey felt complete as she lay in his strong embrace; he said he loved her, and she hoped he meant it. She knew if he didn't, she would never be able to handle it. She closed her eyes, letting the magic of the moment take over all fear. She fell into a deep peaceful sleep knowing tomorrow they would be in Atlanta where all the temptations would be surrounding him. She knew she would need her strength to keep everything in line.

13

JEWEL SAT IN HER HOTEL room, getting ready for the concert. She leaned down towards the table and took a shot of tequila. Throwing her head back, she drank it, letting it burn all the way from her throat to her chest, getting that rush. After a moment of silence, she stood, walked over to her clothes, and slid them over her naked body. The lace of her skintight red mini-dress caused her skin to tingle, and the alcohol heightened her body's senses. After the numbness subsided, she smiled into her mirror. As she watched her reflection, she thought tonight, she would have Nick eating out of the palm of her hand. She could hardly wait to see the shock and pain on Bailey's face when she seduced him.

Jewel-Cora twists the strands of her red hair into snakelike ringlets, knowing how sassy it made her look, especially next to her white complexion. Her lips stood out from the dark red candy-colored lipstick she wore. She grabbed her concert ticket and backstage pass, exited the hotel room. As she strutted from the room, she continued to imagine the shocked looks she would receive from Jax and Kaitlyn tonight. She wondered if Jax's eyes would shine with lust as they did years ago when she walked into a room with him.

Every man in the hotel had their eyes on Jewel as she walked out, her hips swinging seductively back and forth. At the door, she turned to blow them all a kiss. She loved making the men drool.

It was a high even better than the one she got from her drinking. She always loved all the attention she got from all the highest rollers and other men. The only problem was after she regained even a tiny bit of confidence, Jax's face would flash in her mind again and ruin it. No matter what she did or who she met, no one could ever erase the shame he brought her. She flagged down a taxi, hoping inside where she could feel the eyes of the driver on her.

Feeling a bit sassy, Jewel spread her thighs, exposing the patch of red hair between them to the driver that glanced into his mirror at her lustfully. She wet her fingers with the tip of her tongue and slid them between her thighs. She laughed as the driver swerved on the road, getting nervous and all worked up from watching her please her own body. She moaned as she flung her head back, finishing her little teasing game. The driver got more than he bargained for, and she found it utterly exciting.

The nerve-racked cab driver finally reached Jewel's destination; she climbed from the cab, walked to the driver's window, reached inside, kissing him on the mouth. She threw him some cash and walked away to the line of people waiting to go inside the concert. She would have stood there for hours if the bouncer hadn't remembered her from two years back. He called her to the front of the line. "Ey Jewel baby, long time no see. Are you here to get this party started or what?" Jewel smiled; grabbing him by his shaft, she whispered in his ear.

"What do you think?"

Jewel handed the happily surprised bouncer her pass and some cash, then walked inside.

14

NICK SAT BACKSTAGE with Bailey on his lap, straddling him where she rocked her body back and forth, making him grind his teeth. He lifted his bottle of whisky to her pouty lips, and she took a huge drink and kissed him long and hard. The taste of the whiskey mixed with the sweetness of her lips caused his cock to throb, and he bit her bottom lip. Damn, he thought to himself, this woman was everything to him. Bailey took the bottle of whiskey from him, pouring it down her breasts while lifting them to his mouth. He suckled at her, nibbling, tasting the whiskey off of her sweet flesh. "Why don't you put those candy lips on my hard cock, baby," he teased.

Bailey smiled and slid from his lap down to the floor. Nick watched as she unzipped his pants, reached inside, and pulled his pulsating shaft from them. She then wrapped her warm, wet lips tightly around him, beginning to suckle. Nick ran his hand through her golden hair as he continued to watch her. Her mouth caused him to tremble all over with pleasure as words of passion fell from his lips. "Don't stop, woman; show me how much you want to taste me. Make me beg for your body, yeah baby, yeah." Bailey continued to pleasure Nick until she tasted the bittersweetness of his body's juices.

Nick pulled Bailey to her feet and stood up, turning her back to him and bending her over the chair. He pulled her dress to her waist as he drove his thickness into her so savagely that she cried out in both shock and pleasure. Once her body adjusted to the roughness of his thrusts, it began to convulse with intense eroticism. The pleasure took over, and she cried out his name, gripping the chair, spinning into eternal bliss.

A few hours later, Jax stood backstage wearing only his leather pants and boots. He was extremely aroused, a storm of need rushed over him. He bit his lower lip as a growl escaped his throat. He watched Kaitlyn. She was standing across the room, about to slide her red mini-dress over her almost naked body. After accidently hearing Nick and Bailey making love earlier Jax want Kaitlyn with a vengeance. He walked over to her in two long strides.

"Leave it off. Leave the damn dress off," he demanded while unbuttoning his pants. Kaitlyn sighed as she looked into those lust-filled-determined eyes of Jax's. She knew what he wanted from her as he looked at her like a wolf hunting his prey.

Jax brushed Kaitlyn's mouth with his lips, barely restraining himself, afraid he would crush her with the intensity of his need. With a devilish grin, he pulled his long, thick, hardened cock from his pants.

"Jax baby, it's almost show time; you should be getting ready to go on the stage," Kaitlyn sighed. As usual, he didn't listen to her. Dismissing her words; he grabbed her around her waist, pulling her to his body.

"Kaitlyn, I want you to give your man something to think about while he's out there on that stage," he whispered in her ear. He touched her shoulders with his lips, and his hands slid between her thighs, urging her to open them wider. She shivered when she heard his low growl, and her head fell back. His lips slid to her throat. She would have told him to stop if it hadn't been for those skillful fingers of his thrusting deeply into her heated core making her burn with need. Feeling dizzy with passion she finally shook her head all right. Jax stopped his assault on her body senses so she could do as he wanted. He smiled as she slid to her shaky knees and slipped her lips over the tip of his long, strong shaft. Jax leaned against the wall, letting his head fall back as she took him to another world.

Later, Nick and Jax both walked out onto the stage with the band, smiles on their faces. They started playing their guitar and drums as the crowd cheered. "How you doing Atlanta. I'm having a good night;

hope you are too! You metal heads ready to rock," Jax shouted to the audience below as he began to sing.

"Hell yeah," the crowd replied, shouting the band's name over and over again. Always feeling the love, the band rocked it out hard, giving their all for their devoted fans.

Jewel shook her body in the middle of the crowd as she watched Jax and Nick playing and singing. She swore the two of them had become even more handsome in these past two years.

Nick's hair hung down to his shoulders in brown waves now, and he had a beard that made his face look more rugged than it used to. His skin was tanned, and his muscles had gotten a lot bigger, like an Aztec prince on that stage. Oh, how she looked forward to seducing him tonight; she couldn't wait for him to drive his stiff cock deep into her very core of desire. Her gaze left him to glance at Jax. As always, the very sight of him made her heart bleed and her lust rage to dangerous heights. He looked the same, but not as if there was no longer darkness within him. Instead, there was a light and fire that made her desire him all the more. She almost dreaded having to seduce Nick instead of trying to seduce him. However, her need for vengeance outshone her desire, and she again forced her sites on Nick.

After the show, Bailey and Kaitlyn went to the hotel room next to where the band went. They went there to check on little Tristen. His nanny was rocking him when they entered the room. Kaitlyn went up to her smiling and scooped her son from her arms. The nanny smiled and stood up to leave them alone for some privacy. She was a wonderful nanny, and Kaitlyn adored her for that. Bailey watched as she kissed her son on his chubby cheek and sang a lullaby to him. Her heart leaped to her belly. She wondered if she would ever be a mother, and if she were, would she be as good as one as Kaitlyn is to Tristen.

"Is it hard to leave Tristen with a nanny all the time when you attend Jax's concerts," she asked innocently.

Kaitlyn looked up at Bailey and proceeded to answer her questions the

best she could. "I do sometimes wish I could just stay back at our home in San Diego California. The only thing that keeps me from doing so is that I don't want Jax to miss any part of our son's life. I also admit that I do not want him touring alone in case the temptations of the road take over and he slips up as he did in the past before meeting me and having our son," She finishes

rocking Tristen to sleep.

"I don't think Jax would ever do anything to ruin what you two have Kaitlyn. I hope that Nick loves me enough to be that way someday, right now I am not sure I trust him," Bailey sighed. Kaitlyn looked up at her with pity and understanding in her eyes. She knew that her friend was smart not to trust Nick, at least not yet. He was a very complex, and complicated man that feared intimacy and commitment. She did however believe that when he was ready it would be Bailey he ended up with. She saw the love and connection between them, it was just as strong and intense as hers and Jax's. She truly believed if they could overcome all their obstacles and be happy, so could they.

Meanwhile, back in the room, the band was celebrating. Jax and Nick already polished off a bottle of the finest whiskey. The band played and Jax sang for all of their best groupies and friends. Men and women alike watched with much admiration, while everyone danced and celebrated the music. Jewel entered the room like a snake crawling on its belly. She slid her way through the crowd wanting to be sure she was seen by Jax and Nick. All the men's eyes were on her as she stepped up onto a table right in front of the band. She grabbed up a bottle of whiskey drinking it until the bottle became half empty. To get everyone else's attention she dropped the bottle into the floor shattering it into a thousand pieces.

The band stopped playing, and Jax walked up to Jewel, she smiled devilishly her legs stretched out to reveal the luscious length of them. His green eyes scanned her body. She was wearing a skin-tight lace mini-dress that was as red as the blood in his veins. She looked damn good, yet he knew she was like a snake, cold, sneaky, and filled with deadly venom. "What do you want, Jewel," he demanded as he lifted her from the table, pinning her against the wall. He could feel her trembling beneath his hold, doubt more from lust than fear. Jewel always liked it rough-somewhere between the lines of pain and pleasure.

"JAX, PLEASE, I JUST want to make peace with you. I hate the way we ended things, the words of anger that I spoke to you. I know you have no reason on this earth to trust me. I am begging

You to at least hear me out and see what I brought for you as a peace offering," Jewel lied.

Jax loosened his hold on her, and she pulled a bag of Cocaine from between her perky breasts, shaking it in his face.

Jewel smiled inside watching his eager eyes light up, his hands trembled at the sight of his old addiction, and she knew it was just as she suspected he had given it up for Kaitlyn. "Come on Jaxson, you know you want it. Go on, just one little line and you will feel like the God, you know you are," she taunted.

Nick overheard Jewel talking to Jax, so he walked over to where they stood. He exchanged glances with her and then with him. He smiled at Jewel when he saw the bag of coke she dangled in Jax's face. Watching the cold sweat drip from his forehead, he knew Jax was struggling with his old demons. He bit his lip, thinking that one little line would not kill him and that he wouldn't mind a boost himself. The temptation of the drug and the way it would make him feel overrode his feeling of devotion and concern for his friend.

Jewel giggled inside knowing they wouldn't turn down the drugs. She grinned, leaned in, and snorted a line, letting her body go numb. The second the numbness subsided the high kicked in.

"Well do you want it or not," she taunted. Nick smiled and shook his head, yes. Jewel jumped up close to him and sprinkled a line down her arm.

"Wait Nick don't do it. She isn't worth it," Jax hissed. His grabbed Nick's shoulder in an attempt to stop him but it was too late. The line was gone and so was his friend.

"Jewel please," he begged. Jewel laughed, turning her attention back to Jax again. She held the bag of coke up to his face. He flinched his old habits, threatening to take over. His willpower was giving out and his blood beat like a drum in his veins making him shake.

Jax closed his eyes picturing Kaitlyn and Tristen's faces. "No, I don't want it Jewel, get away from me," he hissed through clenched teeth.

Jax's refusal angered her, Jewel reached for the collar of his shirt pulling him into a kiss. He fought her and she slipped the coke into the pocket of his shirt without his noticing. With a snort of satisfaction, she jumped back onto the table shaking her round firm bottom for all in the room to see. An exceedingly high Nick and several men in the room cheered her on as she began to slowly discard her clothes piece by piece.

Nick's manhood hardened in his pants as he looked at Jewel's taunt bright pink nipples that she now bared for all to see. She continued to shake her body sliding her dress to her ankles, kicking it to the floor. She twisted and popped her body wearing no more than her red lace thongs. After she finished her little strip tease, Jewel slid from the table proceeding to walk seductively past Nick and Jax. Her hand motioned for them to follow her.

Jax knew he should stop Nick from following Jewel, but the problem was the cocaine would keep him from thinking straight. He knew he would never listen to reason. He told himself he had to try, so he walked with her and Nick over to the bed. When they reached their destination, Jewel pushed Nick playfully to the mattress. "Jewel, he is high. Stop this; we both know you are only doing this to get at me," Jax accused. She ignored him, climbing onto Nick's lap and twisting, grinding her bottom all over his now-hardened shaft. She turned to smile slyly and Jax, their eyes locked, and she slid her panties off, her bare skin rubbed and teased Nick's manhood.

Jax forced his eyes from Jewel's bare flesh, refusing to be seduced by her games. He reached for her. Jewel gasped as she felt the iron strength of his hands around her waist, pulling her from Nick. As he struggled with her, Nick finally snapped back into reality, thinking of Bailey. He got control back of his body. He stood from the bed, ignoring Jewel's irritated glare. "Jax, let's go," he shouted.

Jax let go of Jewel and turned to his friend. They were about to walk off when she ran up between them. "Alright, I admit it. I was upset, and I wanted to get even. I apologize. Let's have a drink for the past, and I will leave," she swore.

Jax smiled as pleasantly as he could muster, his eyes locking with hers. "I have put what happened between us in the past. I have put you in the past, Jewel."

Jewel lifted her chin in defiance. "I do not believe you, Jax Alan!"

"Well, you should, Red. I love Kaitlyn, and I want only her," Jax hissed.

"I always get what I want in the end, and I warn you, Jax," Jewel looked him straight in the eye.

"I want you or revenge, and I will have one or the other."

"Never," Jax spat, then without waiting for her reply, he walked away.

As he walked back into the middle of the room, he found Kaitlyn looking for him. The minute their eyes locked, Jax knew she knew where he had been. He promised her he wouldn't ever go around Jewel again, yet he had, and the disappointment he saw in her beautiful grey eyes cut him like a knife. She turned from him and ran towards the balcony. "DAMN IT," he cursed out loud as he ran after her.

Bailey hadn't the faintest idea what was with Jax and Kaitlyn, so she continued to scan the room for Nick. Finally, she found him, and what she saw tore her heart. He was lying on

The bed with Jewel on top of him was naked. It was apparent they were close to having intercourse, and she knew she could stop them if she approached them. The problem is she was just so tired of fighting for love to do it. She wanted to turn her gaze on them but was frozen in time. Her once friend would destroy everything between her and the man she loved. She knew Jewel was not interested in Nick; she just wanted to hurt her. Apart from Bailey wanted to know why and how she could be so sadistic, but another part of her just wanted to remain numb to it all.

Jewel turned her head to see Bailey standing in the center of the room, frozen, looking right at her and Nick. The pain she saw in her eyes was bittersweet. Indeed, she knew she had broken her just as she had planned. She turned back, smiling at Nick, glad that he had passed out and that she could make it look like they were hooking up. Even if Jax stung her pride by rejecting her yet again, she felt so justified, so proud of herself for getting her revenge on Bailey. Even when Nick woke up and denied having sex with her, Bailey would never believe him.

Meanwhile, out on the balcony, Jax had problems as he tried desperately to get Kaitlyn to listen to him. "Kaitlyn, I had no idea that this would happen. Please, you have to

believe me." He tried to touch her several times, in which she slapped him or pushed him away

"I don't care! Who gave it to you, Jax? Which groupie whore? Did you sleep with her too," Kaitlyn screamed, her eyes darting to his shirt. Jax followed her eyes to find the bag of cocaine that Jewel must have planted on him, and his anger quickly turned to rage. He grabbed Kaitlyn's arms tightly to pull her to him. Putting his head to hers as he spoke through clenched teeth.

"I love you, but this is a mistake, woman, not mine. I haven't used it in over a year. Jewel tried to give it to me as a peace offering, and I refused. I will never sleep with her again because I love you and our son!"

Kaitlyn stomped Jax's foot, causing his grip on her to loosen; she twisted from him, slapping him hard across the face. "Jewel, you bastard, I hate you," she screamed in his face frantically.

Slamming her fists into his chest, tears streamed all down her face. He grabbed her by her shoulders, shaking her, trying to snap her out of her fit of rage. He wanted to kiss her; she bit his lip.

He was causing it to bleed. "Damn it, Kaitlyn," he said as he let go of her again, and she stormed from him back into the hotel to find Bailey standing frozen in the middle of the room.

Kaitlyn's gaze followed hers as she saw Jewel and Nick in bed together. Her heart bled for Bailey, so she approached her. Bailey turned to see her next to her, and she let all her pain spring forth, flinging herself into Kaitlyn's arms. "Let's go check on Tristen. Let Jax and Nick play with the tramp," Kaitlyn cried, wanting to get out of there and away from Jewel before she did something she would regret.

Bailey took one last look at Nick and walked away. Jewel smiled, seeing the look in Kaitlyn's eyes, knowing she had just killed two birds with one stone. It was clear that they were finished with both Nick and Jax. She smiled as she climbed from the bed where Nick was still passing so he wouldn't find her there when he woke up. She wished she could be a fly on the wall when they fought over her, but knowing it was impossible, she decided to settle for the pleasure of knowing she had ended their happiness.

Jax slammed his fists into the balcony's brick wall and screamed curses. He had never seen Kaitlyn so angry with him. He feared that she would now want to leave him, and he knew he would die without her and his son. He knew he would never let her go, even if that meant he would have to keep her prisoner. She was and always would be his for all eternity as

It was their son. He decided to stay on the balcony for the night and try to get through to her in the morning. Damn Jewel and her devious plotting; why now, he wondered sourly. Why, after two years, did she show up here tonight and try to seduce him back into the world of drugs and darkness? He wanted to strangle the frolicsome bitch, but what good would it do now that the damage was done. Jewel was a devious monster; this was true, but Jax could not help but feel he was at least partially responsible for what she became. He would leave it alone and try to fix the damage between him and his beautiful lotus flower. Kaitlyn and their son were all that mattered now.

16

Nick woke up, his head pounding; he rolled over to find himself naked. Jewel was sitting on the bed next to him with a devious grin on her face. The memories of the night before flowed through his head. "Damn it," he cursed, jumping from the bed frantically, pulling his pants back up. He instantly regretted taking the cocaine from her and letting himself be seduced into whatever vicious game she was playing with him. He wished he had listened to Jax when he tried to warn him not to trust her.

Jewel laughed. Nick's look was like music to her heart; now, all she had to do was sit back and watch the disaster she had caused unfold. She felt a bit of gratification, knowing that they would all suffer, as she had for years now. She could finally find a little peace, knowing all her despair was no longer in vain. Ashes, ashes, it was past time they all fell, burning in the flames of her fiery fury.

Nick wanted desperately to slap the hell out of Jewel; however, finding Bailey is most important to him now. He stalked across the room, his eyes scanning the place for her. When he saw she was not in the room, he went out to the balcony outside. There, he found Jax passed out, leaning against the wall. He bent down and gently shook him; Jax jumped up, looking at Nick.

"What all happened last night? Why are you out here? Where's Kaitlyn and Bailey?" Nick asked.

"What do you think happened? Kaitlyn found out Jewel was here, and she thinks I've not only cheated on her but I used drugs again. It seems, my friend, that she must have told Bailey about it, or you let that seductress have her way with you, and your woman saw it. It appears that you and I have messed up again," Jax replied, irritated by the thought of being set up by Jewel. He pushed Nick aside and stormed into the hotel to confront the little vicious cunt. He would get answers out of her if he had to shake them from her. He spotted her almost instantly; the look in her eyes told him she was waiting for him, too.

Jewel stood against the wall when she saw Jax storming right at her. She could see the fire burning in his green eyes. She knew this would happen, and she even waited here deliberately so he could find her. She had to see him one last time before letting him go for good; his rage would help her cut the ties. She tensed as he grew closer with each step he took in her direction. She cried out in pain when he grabbed her by her throat, his large-powerful hands tightening in his growing anger.

"I swear if you did this on purpose, I would kill you," he hissed.

Jewel stood there with a blank expression, so proud of being the cause of Jax's rage and desperation. She thought how badly he must want to hit her, to make her pay for his mistakes. A part of herself that was dark and lost wished for him to strike her and make her feel physical pain. She sickly thought perhaps the physical would override the emotional. Slightly broken was she, but somehow, his grasp on her throat made her heart bleed for pain and pleasure. She bit her lower lip so hard it bled as she awaited his next move.

Nick rushed into the room when he saw Jax holding Jewel by the throat. "Jax, she isn't worth it. We need to concentrate on Kaitlyn and Bailey. They are priority ones. She is nothing," he insisted. His breath faltered as he waited, hoping his words would reach Jax and get his wild temper to wane before he did something he would regret. He closed his eyes in relief when he saw him loosen his cast iron grip on Jewel's throat.

Knowing how right Nick was, Jax let Jewel go, not bothering to even give her a last glance. He turned from her and followed him out of the room, forgetting she existed. As he exited, he hoped she felt his rejection so deeply it branded her for the rest of her miserable life. He prayed she finally accepted that she no longer meant anything to him. She was a distant memory that he chose to distinguish forever.

Jax and Nick went to Tristen's room, hoping to find Kaitlyn and Bailey, but the door was locked. "Kaitlyn, open the damn door now," Jax shouted. Kaitlyn and Bailey paced the room at the sound of Jax's demand. His voice made it crystal clear that all the play was out of him, and he would get inside one way or the other.

"What are you going to do, Kaitlyn?" Bailey whispered, fearing the door would be damaged if she did not open it and let Jax inside.

"I don't know. I want to avoid Jax at all costs; I need time to think," Kaitlyn sighed.

Bailey did not have a chance to reply. She could hear Nick yelling for her to please open the door and talk to him. She tried to drown him out by closing her eyes and thinking of anything else but him and how badly he hurt her. "I want to avoid Nick too. I wish I hadn't ever let him back in my heart or bed," she cried.

Nick and Jax lost their tempers; they decided they weren't about to stand here knocking on the damn door. They stormed off to head to the front desk and demanded the extra key. They didn't care if they had to bribe the lady out of the key they would get in that room. The lady behind the desk smiled sweetly when Jax asked her for her aid. "My wife lost our room key, and I wanted to do something special for her. Can you assist me," he grinned boyishly. The clerk smiled and nodded, handing him a key without hesitation. They stormed back to the hotel room to unlock the door.

"When we get in here, you might want to take Bailey somewhere else to talk. I am going to show Kaitlyn, who is wearing the pants," Jax told Nick.

"Good luck with that, Jax; you know how stubborn Kaitlyn can be," Nick teased.

Bailey and Kaitlyn stood frozen as they heard the lock turning in the door, knowing their men would be boiling with rage. The door swung open wide, and they walked inside. Jax looked directly at

Tristen's nanny. "Take my son to the bus, Melissa," he ordered. The nanny turned red, doing exactly as he asked without a single question.

"Jax, I'm not going with you on tour, nor are Tristen or Bailey. We have decided we'll catch a plane to San Diego tomorrow," Kaitlyn said in a shaky voice. Jax crossed the room and grabbed her before she finished speaking.

Nick stood for the longest time, just looking at Bailey. She looked defeated, as if she had given up on everything that mattered to her. In her eyes, there was no anger, only despair. "Bailey, I never meant to hurt you. I said I loved you, and I swear I still do. We belong together. I realize this now; there's no turning back. Don't let my mistake of trusting Jewel cost us what we share. She set me up. I never touched her," he pleaded.

Bailey looked deep into Nick's brown eyes, and she could see all the love and pain in them. She knew he meant all he just said to her. The problem was she was so scared of being hurt again that she ran past him without a single word. She hated leaving Kaitlyn alone with them, but she could not face Nick at that moment. Every time she looked at him, she would see him and Jewel in that bed. It was too hard to believe that it was a setup. She could hear Nick behind her as she continued to run, and by the time she reached the elevator, it was too late; she had nowhere else to go.

Nick threw both his hands up on each side of her, pinning her to the wall. "Don't run from your feelings for me, Bailey. I know you think I cheated and that I ruined everything, but I swear nothing happened. Please believe me!" Tears ran from Bailey's eyes as she looked up at him, to see the tears in his eyes, too.

Bailey's heart hammered in her chest, and she let it take control of her emotions. "Kiss me, Nick, hold me, don't ever let me go, make me forget what I thought I saw," she cried as she threw her arms around his neck. Nick seized the moment and kissed her deeply as the elevator door opened; he backed her inside, where his lips continued to taste hers. He was letting her see a side of himself that he dared never show to anyone else. This woman was changing him and for once he refused to let his fear ruin it. Bailey's hands frantically unbuttoned his pants, and his lips left hers, traveling down to her neck, where he tasted the flesh of her warm body.

Nick's lips were so warm on her chilled flesh that it sent tremors all through Bailey's body until she ached for his hands to touch her all over. She slid her trembling hands down his pants and caressed his erection, making it harden in her soft hands. It felt so warm and hard yet soft and inviting that she wanted to taste it. She slid to her knees and began to suckle at him until she felt his shaft throb in her mouth. Nick pulled her to her feet, nibbling at the tender flesh of her nipples through the fabric of her dress, where they quickly became hard with need. Wanting to feel them in his mouth, he pulled her dress down to her waist, where his gaze slid all across her body; she was the most desirable woman he had ever known. Her breasts were so round, so firm, her nipples such a light pink that they almost seemed to stand out from the rest of her luscious body.

Nick lowered his lips to Bailey's beautiful nipples, kissing them as his tongue slid back and forth, and the warm wetness of his tongue caused her to cry out. Her breath became ragged as his warm hands slid her dress the rest of the way down her body. After discarding Bailey's clothes and leaving her naked, Nick stood back, taking his pants off. "Look at me, Bailey. I want you to see how much I desire you. How much I love you when I make love to you here and now."

Bailey sucked in a deep breath as she looked upon his naked flesh, thinking he was so handsome, from his long dark hair, brown eyes, his long muscular legs. Just looking at him made her body burn with need. She held her arms open to him as he approached her. He kissed her savagely, and she wrapped her legs around him tightly. She grabbed his throbbing shaft and guided it deep inside her welcoming body. "Take me, Nick, take me now, and see in my eyes that I return your love tenfold," she moaned.

At Bailey's request, Nick became lost in passion, thrusting deep into her tight, warm body. She felt so good he swore he could die in her arms and be ultimately at peace with it. His body shook with intense pleasure at the repeated cry of his name that escaped her lips with each. powerful thrust of his cock inside her thicket of heated honey. Her body exploded with sweet release. The tightening of it on his passion-filled erection caused him to fill her to the core with his hot seed.

Meanwhile, back in the hotel room, Jax and Kaitlyn argued over her not wanting to go on tour with him. "Kaitlyn, you are my reason to breathe. I refuse to leave you or our son behind," Jax

Insisted.

"Ya, well I refuse to watch the man I love slip back into his old habits and lose everything that makes him the man I fell in love with. I love you way too much to watch you fall. It would kill me," Kaitlyn fired back. Jax pulled her into his arms, kissing her so passionately that she wilted in his embrace.

Jax's kisses soon became caresses that sent Kaitlyn spinning into a world of desire. A desire that burned her deep inside, making her nether region ache for his shaft inside of her. Jax heard himself utter a groan of relief and need. He had to be inside of her immediately, his muscles quivered with tension at the sensations her body brought to his. He retook her lips and kissed her fiercely, swallowing her cries of pleasure, pouring every bit of passion he had into her. Shuddering, he lowered himself and her to the floor, taking her with great love and unbridled passion. Afterward, he held her in his arms until his heart stopped pounding and his breathing slowed. As he held her, Jax knew he had to make this night up to her, that he almost messed up everything between them. He smiled to himself, thinking how lucky he was to have friends everywhere he went. He would call in a little favor and give Kaitlyn a night she would never forget.

17

Jax's eyes scanned the room, content that everything was perfectly in place for tonight. The rose petals were scattered in a trail from the threshold of the door through the entire room, leading first to a hot bath, scented with rose oil and colored pink by petals in the water and then to the bed dressed in red satin sheets. He ran the palm of his hand across the pink silk dress he

I bought it for her, especially tonight, remembering how her eyes lit up when he gave it to her that afternoon. He closed his eyes, envisioning her wearing it as he danced with her out on the

Balcony sang the song he had written for her as they danced. Jax's vision was interrupted when he heard a faint knock at the door; his heart raced, and Kaitlyn was finally here. He turned and

He walked to the door and opened it to find her standing there, her beautiful grey eyes puzzled.

"What are you up to now, Jax Alan?"

"Please come in and find out, my love," Jax teased. Kaitlyn glanced at the floor before them from his handsome face and twinkling eyes. Her breath caught in her throat at the sight of the rose petals on the floor. She looked back into his emerald-like eyes, letting him slide his arm around her waist, lifting her off her feet. He carried her across the threshold as a groom would his bride, and it melted her heart like the flames of a candle melted wax. Her tear-stained eyes took in the beauty of the room and all he had done to it, the rose petals and candles, the soft music that played like the whispering of the wind in the background. She trembled in his strong arms as he carried her past the bed to the bath, where he set her down gently to her feet. She stood on her tiptoes, sliding her trembling hand around his neck, pulling him into a loving kiss.

"Jax, I don't know what to say; I love you. This means so much to me, my love," Kaitlyn's voice cracked with emotion.

Jax smiled sweetly and brushed his thumb across Kaitlyn's soft lips. He then kissed her back, sliding his hand further to caress her tear-stained cheek. His eyes never left hers as his hands continued to slide further down to her throat, across her shoulders to her waist, lifting her shirt over her shoulders and head. Their love and heated passion lit up the entire room as he continued to remove her clothing piece by piece until she was left nude, trembling in need before him. Again, his arms slid around her waist to lift her from the floor.

"Jax," she whispered as he lowered her into the hot tub. "Are you not going to join me in the bath?"

"No, baby. Tonight is all about your pleasure. I want everything to be completely perfect, Kaitlyn. You are my wife in every way that matters; everything else is just paper. Tonight, I show you how much I love and need you," Jax whispered.

Kaitlyn's only reply was a single tear sliding down her cheek, a tear he kissed away as fast as it fell. The rose oil teased her nostrils, making them flare as Jax began to wash her. The feel of his solid but soft hands slid across first her shoulders and back, then her breasts, making her blood run hot and her pulse dance. She moaned. She watched the lines of his face change with each caress he bestowed upon her naked flesh. His jaw flexed, and she knew how difficult it was for him to restrain himself. She smiled, deciding to take full advantage of his romantic side. Her head rolled back to lay against his bare chest as he continued to wash her. By the time he had her fully bathed, she was burning with intense need, dying for him to make love to her.

Jax's eyes darkened with animalistic lust and desire as he lifted Kaitlyn from the water and began to dry her damp flesh. He slid the towel from her wet hair, down her throat and shoulders, across her breasts. Her nipples puckered, and he growled. He bit hard into his lip, tasting his coppery blood in his mouth, forcing his control to remain steady. He could smell the musky scent of her passion as he lowered the towel further down across her thighs, down her long legs. His eyes rolled back in his head; his inner darkness threatened to consume him.

"Jax, breathe," Kaitlyn teased, her hand running sweetly through the locks of his blonde hair. He looked up into her eyes, and his control calmed again. He finished drying her quickly.

Kaitlyn's heart pounded like a drum as she let Jax lead her from the bathroom to their bed. She was more than ready for him to take her. She let out a breath of air and a sigh when, instead of leading her down to the bed, he lifted the dress he gave her and slid it over her naked body. The satin fabric teased at her flesh, tickling her nipples, and they strained painfully against it. Jax let out a small laugh, and her heart skipped a beat. He was breathtaking tonight, too handsome for mere words. He held his hand out to her; she smiled and took it without hesitation, letting him lead her again; this time, their destination was the balcony. Her eyes lit up when they caught sight of the table in the center of it: candles, strawberries, cream cheese, and wine. If she didn't already love him, she would have fallen in love then and there.

Kaitlyn watched Jax in admiration and love. He walked over to one side of the table and pulled her chair out for her. She strolled on unsteady legs and sat in the chair, chuckling when he

She first kissed her cheek, then pushed her chair in for her. He sat across from her and dipped a juicy strawberry into the cream cheese. His eyes were full of amusement when he lifted the dessert to her lips. Kaitlyn opened her mouth, and her tongue slid up to circle the sweetness of the strawberry. She bit softly into the juicy fruit and swallowed, more than a little pleased to see the amusement in Jax's eyes fade away to be replaced by raw, untamed desire. She continued to let him feed her, seducing him slowly with her lips and tongue, letting the juice of the fruit tease her taste buds deliciously.

Jax thought he would go mad if he didn't kiss Kaitlyn's lips; he stood from his end of the table and reached her in one stride. She moaned as he leaned in and brushed his lips against hers, licking the excess wine and strawberries from her lips. His warm tongue danced with hers seductively. Their kiss did not last nearly long enough as far as Kaitlyn was concerned. She longed for him to make love to her on the balcony floor.

"Dance with me, wife of my heart; dance with your husband," Jax asked in a strained voice. Kaitlyn's heart turned to liquid silver. She took his hand, and they danced in the moon's light. Jax sang the song of her heart as they swayed in perfect unison, making this night the most romantic night of their last two years together.

18

Jewel nearly exploded with rage when she saw Kaitlyn and Bailey get on the tour bus with the band, all walking hand in hand. She swore she would find another way to get at them all, even if she had to go to Druid Hills, where Kaitlyn was from, and dig up something. She knew there had to be a reason no one knew Kaitlyn's last name except for her, Nick, Bailey, and Jax. Jewel wondered if Kaitlyn's father had something to do with all of it. Her memory of the night Jax brought Kaitlyn back with him and turned her out went through her mind. Kaitlyn had been bruised and battered when Jax came into the hotel room with her in his arms. Jewel knew the answer to bringing Jax to his knees would be found in Georgia.

Jewel walked away from the hotel, determined to round up enough cash to get a plane ticket to Druid Hills. She was half-owner of her strip club, where she still danced but knew that her partner would never let her dip into the till for money. She smiled devilishly as she remembered a few of the men who were willing to pay her for a good time. Men who frequented the club. She decided she would dance tonight for a few hundred and then play naughty for a few hundred more. It never seized her to amaze her how easily men were led into giving her what she wanted by a mere touch of her heated body against theirs.

Jewel flagged down a taxi and hopped inside. "Take me to the pleasure palace on the strip," she demanded. She watched the busy people walking from here and there from the window of her taxi, but her mind flowed back to another time and place.

Jewel was twenty again at the first strip club she ever worked at. When she had her first night as one of the exotic dancers. The first night, she saw Jax in the flesh. He was sitting at a table alone, drinking a bottle of whiskey. His handsomeness stole her breath from her lungs. When her eyes met him, he made her feel a desire she never knew existed. A desire she hadn't felt again since he threw her away. She nervously stood backstage after pacing for hours, knowing he would watch her dance. She bit her lip as the curtain opened, and her music filled the club. She ran up to the pole in the center of the stage and looked into Jax's emerald-green eyes. She had danced for him alone, ignoring everyone in the club. He smiled, and she lost her balance, falling to the floor. To add to her shame, he stood up and walked away.

A single tear slid down Jewel's cheek as she forced this painful memory and so many more from her mind. Jax had often hurt her, yet she still loved him despite it all. She knew she must force this love from her heart, turn it into only bitterness. Turn the love into rage even if she had to remember the most painful memory of them all. The memory of their love child. Her sweet little Lantana and how she had given her away. She wondered what Kaitlyn would think if she knew Jax had fathered another child. A child with her. She wondered what he would think or if he would even care. At the thought of her forever-lost child, all her love for Jax went sour again. She closed her eyes, fighting the urge to cry.

Jewel was relieved when her taxi stopped, letting her know she had reached the club. She paid the driver and quickly exited the cab. She smiled at the other dancers as they greeted her, and she asked if she was dancing tonight. She told them she would not have it any other way. Without another word, she entered the dressing room. She went to the costume closet and picked out a red lace corset. She pulled her dress over her head and replaced it with the corset. She tossed her head up and down several times to give her red hair a sexy look that would make all the male customers think of sex. With a content smile on her lips and a quick wink in the mirror at her reflection, she was ready to dance.

Jewel walked out onto the stage. The lights burned hot as she danced; her body swayed in perfect unison with the music. She smiled, watching the many men in her club throw money up at her and slide ones into the loop of her guarder. Their hungry eyes feasted on the exposed flesh of her body. She danced for an hour, and the stage floor was covered with money. She grinned, knowing she must have made at least a few hundred. The moment the music of her last song ended, she collected every dollar on the stage and exited.

Later, in her hotel room, she was pleased to find that she had made five hundred tonight, much more than expected. She was delighted that she would not have to entertain any more men to get more money; this money from dancing was just enough. She gathered her cash and threw it in her bag, heading out to purchase her plane ticket to Georgia.

Hours later, Jewel boarded the plane to Georgia. From there, she planned to rent a car and drive to Druid Hills; she did just this when she left the hotel. Once seated, her mind wandered back to past events once again.

On the night Jax had shown up with Kaitlyn back at the hotel, they again remembered how Kaitlyn had been beaten. Her lip was split, and she had several bruises on her face. Her father had done all of it to her. The question was how Jax got her from him without the police's involvement.

What had happened back there that Kaitlyn left all her life behind without a single thought? Jewel knew this would be the key to bringing Bailey to her knees. Later, she looked up Kaitlyn's father's name and address at the Druid Hills library. Her eyes grew wide as she saw the words deceased on his information. She read on to discover he had been murdered the same night Jax went after Kaitlyn. She read on to find that his murder remained unsolved and that the daughter was only notified by phone because she was at the dorms at the time he was murdered. I've got you now, Jewel thought to herself as she stood to leave. It all came crystal clear to her now: Jax killed Kaitlyn's father in self-defense, and knowing Kaitlyn was pregnant, he fled to stay out of jail.

Jewel knew Bailey would do anything to protect Kaitlyn and that she'd do it if she told her to leave Nick forever. She would do it to keep her from they are exposing Kaitlyn and Jax. "Owe isn't love grand," Jewel laughed. She couldn't wait to go back and blackmail Bailey into leaving Nick, the only man she would ever love. Together, they would be as bitter and lost as before meeting the men they loved, who swept them into a world of passion and love. It seemed they had always been destined to walk the same vindictive path in this world of nothingness. She knew this was doing Bailey a favor by forcing her to accept this fate that belonged to them.

19

Nick smiled sweetly as he watched Bailey step from his limo in the golden evening gown he bought her. She was the most beautifully seductive lioness he'd ever known, and he was damn proud to have her as his woman. He took her small hand and raised it to his lips for a soft kiss upon her palm. " Ready for a romantic evening, my angel," he teased.

"I have never been more ready for anything than I am to be here with you at this very moment," Bailey smiled. Her smile made Nick's heart race; he sucked in an uneven breath and led her towards the restaurant. Her hand squeezed his tight in anxiety as all eyes were on her when she entered the restaurant on his arm, making her slightly nervous.

"Stop shaking, angel. You are being stared out in admiration, not at anything else. You are remarkably stunning in that dress."

"Nick, you always know what to say," Bailey whispered, her nerves starting to calm. She loosened her hold on his hand and let him lead her further inside together. They were seated at a table at the very edge of the room. They sat down, and she relaxed enough to let her eyes take in the room's beauty. The tables were red oak with roses hand-carved on their surface, and the chairs were the same, with white silk seats. Her eyes looked up at the light that hung like moons above the tables, shining like gems in the sun's rays. The place was class A and fit for a queen.

It made her feel like she was worth something again. Her mind was jumping with thoughts and memories of more challenging times when she felt Nick's warm hand reach for hers.

"Do you like it? I hope it is a yes because I want to give you the absolute best, Bailey, and it doesn't get any better than this," Nick whispered warmly.

"Like isn't even the word; you will spoil me, Bailey blushed."

"Isn't that the point, angel? Let's order; you can have anything you like." Nick smiled. Bailey sighed, took the menu, and read it slowly. She wanted to order something elegant but full of flavor. She looked up to see amusement in Nick's eyes, making her blush. She quickly chose a seafood chef salad and blueberry cheesecake as her meal.

"I think I will have the same. After all, Jax is always teasing that I need to watch what I eat before I get out of shape," Nick laughed, hoping his humor would help Bailey thaw out a little more. He wanted her to have a good time. He waved his left hand at the waiter, gave the polite gentlemen their order, and handed him a large tip.

Bailey felt nothing could ruin her happiness again while she ate her dinner with Nick. He would look up from his plate now and then to give her a smile that melted her heart.

"Well, Darling, dinner was great, but I have something much better planned. If you are finished here, we can be on our way," Nick asked with a wolfish grin.

"I am not sure my mind can take in much more, Nick; you have already left me breathless with Dinner," Bailey sighed. Nick loved that he was making a decent impression on Bailey. He wanted to make the past up to her and win her heart like no other. He grinned at her more comprehensively, pushed his chair back, and stood, walking over to her side of the table. He held his hand out to her.

"Come on, Bailey, live a little with me. There are still a few things you don't know about me."

"Now, what might that be, Nick? Hmm. Now, I am intrigued. Surprise me," Bailey laughed, taking his hand and letting him help her stand. Together, they walked from the restaurant, looking like newlyweds, their faces aglow with love and laughter.

Bailey looked at Nick inside the vehicle, wondering where he was taking her. She detected a hint of mischief in his eyes. She wanted to question him but knew he would never give as much as a clue. She smiled at him, inching closer, running her hand up his chest, across his shoulders until reaching his neck, where she slid her fingers back and forth across his warm flesh.

She gives her best seducer look, and he grits his teeth in desire; she giggles.

"Come on, babe, just one tiny hint," Bailey begged.

"Alright, Baby. I am taking you dancing, my sweet."

"Dancing, umm Nick, wait a minute, I mean, what if someone at the club knows me from..." Bailey's voice trailed off.

"Not that kind of dancing, baby doll. I am taking you to a ballroom dance hall, not some club. Bailey, I want tonight to be romantic for you. I thought it was a lovely slow dance in a calm environment. It would be an excellent way to spend time together."

"Oh, Nick, I am sorry. I didn't mean to; I'd love to go," Bailey smiled in embarrassment. Her face turned crimson, and her eyes shot to the ground. She felt so stupid for ruining their night.

With the shame of her career. She felt tears threatening her eyes until she felt the warm, soft caress of Nick's hand upon her chin, lifting her face back up so her eyes again met his.

"Bailey, never look down on anyone, especially me. I am damn proud to be with you. I don't care what you did or do as a career. I love you because you are you; never doubt that. How about we dance for a while and forget the world?" Bailey's heart swelled with love and pride. She kissed Nick long and hard, shaking her head yes to the ballroom.

20

Nick sat backstage with Jax and the rest of their band, watching Bailey. They had a wonderful romantic dinner only hours before, and he wished they were still there. She was so beautiful; just looking at her took his breath away and made him want to spoil her as he did today for the rest of her natural days. She wore a black leather mini-dress that fit snugly over her body tonight. The outfit was showing off every luscious curve. He told her time and time again how much he loved her, yet looking at her now, he felt the need to say to her again. He constantly found little ways to prove his love and desire for her. For example, when the media asked him who she was, he said she was his soul. The only woman for him. He knew he would never forget how her eyes sparkled at those words.

Nick took a hit from his cigarette while watching his soulmate. She helped him overcome his fears of settling down and the fear he would have to change himself. Bailey partied harder than any of the bands in the past two months. Afterward, she would become her tame, loving self, and they would make love night after a passionate night. At these times, he realized that she was the only woman for him. She did not know it yet, but she would be his wife; he'd already asked Jax to be the best man. He only had to ask her now and planned to do so after tonight's show. He could hardly wait to see the look in her crystal blue eyes, knowing she would never see it coming. It would be amusing to watch her freak out and then say yes.

Bailey looked up from fixing her hair to find Nick's eyes on her. In those eyes, she saw his raw love and desire for her. She knew he finally loved her as much as she always loved him. She smiled warmly at him, thinking of how he'd fought these emotions for so long to only give into them now. Wanting to be next to him, she stood and walked in his direction, swinging her curvy hips to get his attention even more.

Nick's shaft shifted in his leather pants as he watched Bailey's hips sway. She was so seductive that it drove him insane. He could hardly wait to spend the rest of his life with this woman. He was going to worship her like some Greek Princess. He laid his drumstick down, grinning as she straddled his lap. He pulled her head down for a gentle kiss, wanting to tease her before giving her what he knew she desperately wanted. Bailey suddenly slid her hand down the front of his pants, caressing his shaft, stroking it as gently as he tasted her trembling lips. It would seem she had plans of her own.

Bailey could feel Nick's thickness hardening in her hand as the veins pumped rapidly. She loved how their bodies seemed to belong together whenever they made love. She moaned hoarsely as she felt the caress of his strong hand sliding her dress up to her waist. She sucked in a deep breath; he began to caress her warm, welcoming neither region over the fabric of her black satin panties. Her hand frantically grabbed his, guiding it inside the front of her panties. She wanted to feel his magic fingers deep inside her wanton body, making her shake with intense need.

Nick nearly lost control of the warm wetness of Bailey's nether regions; his breath came in long pants as he reached around her to grab her round, firm ass. He stood, lifting her with him, and carried her over to a table in the room. He laid her down on it and pulled his throbbing manhood from his confining pants, letting it spring forth with an insane need to divide and conquer. Bailey followed his lead, shedding her remaining clothes and parting her thighs as he thrust forward to enter her welcoming body.

"Nick, my love, my soul, oh Nick," she cried ecstatically. Bailey knew in this very moment that if she lived for all eternity, she would never love or desire a man the way she desired and loved him.

Nick swore he would die from the intense pleasure Bailey's body gave him each time he took her. He continued to thrust into her luscious body over and over again, making her shake with tremors of raw passion, causing the flames of desire to grow to tremendous heights. The feel of her womanly core squeezing his shaft caused him to spill his warm seed deep within her. He swore that no other woman ever made him feel so alive, so free yet connected simultaneously. It was as if fate had blown her to him from across the oceans of time and space so they could meet and become one.

Jewel remained hidden in the closet of the backstage room, where she watched Bailey and Nick make love. She could see that the love they shared was pure. Too bad she was about to crush it with just a few words, she thought silently as she waited for Bailey to be alone. The moment finally came when she saw Nick pull his pants back up over his hips and pull Bailey into a long, soft kiss, then leave to join the band.

"Bailey, Legs, we meet again," Jewel hissed.

Bailey nearly jumped from her skin when she heard Jewel call her name. She turned to find her standing right behind her. Her first thought was to slap the fire out of her, grab her by that red hair, and throw her out of there. Before she could act on her instincts, Jewel spoke again.

"I want you to walk out on Nick tonight. It's time for you to feel the same desperation that I felt when I lost Jax two years ago." Bailey laughed at Jewel and tried to walk past her, but her laughter seized at Jewel's following words.

"I would not laugh if I was you, Legs. Remember how Kaitlyn was kidnapped by her father? I know what happened. I swear on everything unholy that if you don't do as I ask, I will destroy her. I have everything I need to ruin Kaitlyn and Jax for the rest of their lives."

"Do you want their boy in foster care?" Jewel finished and laughed inside when Bailey's face grew as pale as snow. She threw the newspaper clippings at her, daring her to deny the truth. When Bailey stood in awkward silence, she continued.

"I will expose Kaitlyn's true identity and that Jax killed her minister father. So, tell me, what's it going to be, huh? Leave Nick or destroy your friend?"

Jewel grinned proudly. "You have until morning to answer me," she warned.

Bailey could feel her world spinning out of control. She sat on the bed, her legs too weak to support her weight. "Jewel, why are you doing this to me? We were once friends?"

"I blame you for losing Jax to Kaitlyn. Jax would have married me if it weren't for you trading me in for her. I want you to finally admit that we are two of a kind and destined to be alone. We are cursed to walk this world side by side in hell," Jewel answered angrily.

Bailey does not get to deny Jewel's words because she turns and walks out of the room without even glancing her way. Bailey's heart was torn between protecting Kaitlyn and her son and being with the only man she would ever love. She knew that no matter which choice she made, it would kill her deep inside and destroy her heart and soul. She knew that if Jewel went to the police, not only would Jax go to prison, but they would lose little Tristen forever. Her heart bled, and she realized she had no choice at all. The only thing she could do was walk away from Nick and never look back. She must do this to protect the people she loves the most.

21

Kaitlyn kissed Nick on the cheek and hugged him. "I am so incredibly happy for you. Bailey will make you a wonderful wife. She will be so thrilled when you ask her." Nick smiled at her with warmth and compassion in his eyes.

"You know we could make it a double wedding. Isn't it about time you and Jax get hitched yourselves?" he teased. Kaitlyn bit her lower lip as Nick continued to go on and on about how he thought Jax and her should have tied that knot by now, how he did not understand what could hold them back when they loved each other so fiercely.

Kaitlyn glanced over to where Jax stood; their eyes locked; she could see all the pain in his. It was evident that he was saying sorry. She smiled back at him, her silent way of saying she was happy just being by his side and that she loved him and knew he loved her. She wanted to ensure he knew that this was enough; it would always be enough.

Jax smiled back, understanding what her smile meant. However, somewhere deep inside, he felt that she needed—hell, deserved—so much more.

Nick was utterly confused by the looks he saw in Jax and Kaitlyn's eyes. He had never really thought about any of it before. How odd they were about her and her past at times. How Kaitlyn never revealed her last name to any of them. She never mentioned what happened the night Jax brought her back from her father's home. He shook his head, turned, and walked out onto the stage, figuring they would have said something by now if they wanted him to know the truth. He decided to mind his business and just let it go.

When Nick went to the stage, Jax pulled Kaitlyn into his arms. He lifted her head to look into her sad eyes. "Are you sure you are all right with all of this? The fact is that we can never wed. Are you going to be all right with Nick and Bailey getting engaged? That it won't cause you to long for us to be?" He asked softly.

"I want you to know and believe that if there were a way anyway that was safe, I would marry you right here and now. You are my life, Kaitlyn, always."

Kaitlyn smiled at the sweetness of Jax's words and how his calm, husky voice soothed her, melting her heart and soul. "Bailey's happiness means the world to me. Jax. You are my husband in my heart, and you always will be. I do not need a paper to prove it." Her heart swelled with such emotion that she thought it would burst when he kissed her long and hard before walking out onto the stage with Nick and the rest of his band. She walked over to Tristen, leaned down, picked him up, and exited the room to see Bailey. She couldn't imagine what was keeping her.

Kaitlyn knew seeing Bailey would help her feel less disappointed that she would never be Jax's wife in name. She hated being punished for her father's wickedness. If he hadn't tried to kill her, he would be alive now, and she would be Jax's wife. She sometimes wished they had gone to the authorities that night. However, she knew Jax had been right. They would have locked him up, refusing to believe a minister would be so evil.

Bailey tore the paper clipping Jewel gave her to shreds and flushed it when Kaitlyn entered the room. She turned, forcing a smile. She couldn't let Kaitlyn see her pain. She reached her hands out to hold Tristen. Kaitlyn handed him to her, and she took him in her arms and kissed him on his chubby cheek. She wanted to spend as much time with him and Kaitlyn before leaving them behind. She wanted them to know how much she loved them and always would, even if they never saw her again.

Meanwhile, Nick played his drums onstage, thinking of how beautiful Bailey would be on their wedding day and how she had given him peace in his rock and roll life. He knew he belonged to her; no other woman would ever be in his blood, heart, and soul the way she was. He knew it was the same for her, too, that she loved him and only him. He also knew what it was like for Kaitlyn and Jax. Once again, he was puzzled as to why they had never gotten married. With all of this on his mind, he finished the show.

22

KAITLYN AND BAILEY kissed Tristen, laid him in his crib, and left to join the band backstage. Once there, they could see a party going on. Everyone was either singing with a drink or dancing to the music the band now played for them all. Even after all this time, seeing Jax perform took Kaitlyn's breath away. He must have felt her eyes on him, for he looked at her smiling, stopped playing his guitar, and motioned her over to him. As an enslaved person obeys its master, Kaitlyn obeyed her man, walking straight to him.

Bailey knew by the looks exchanged between Jax and Kaitlyn that she would have all the time she needed with Nick tonight. She was thankful for this, knowing tonight would be her last night with him. At this moment, their eyes locked; Nick continued to play his drums as if he were playing the very beat of her heart. He played the very strings of her heart with each thud on the drum. She swore she would take the memory of tonight with her for all her living days. No matter how miserable her life became, she would remember how he looked at her that night.

Nick stopped playing, laid his drumsticks down, and walked to Bailey, pulling her into his strong, protective arms. His lips lowered to press firmly upon her; the kiss was pure love and unbridled passion. Bailey could feel tears threatening to fill her eyes. She pushed them back, promising she would make this night a night neither could ever forget. She slid her trembling hand through his hair and kissed him back desperately.

Nick smiled as he thought of the perfect spot to propose to Bailey. He took her hand, leading her from the room. She followed him out into the hall, and he turned her to face him. His eyes searched her lovingly. "I have a surprise for you, Bailey. I must blindfold you. Is that alright?" he asked. Bailey smiled back and nodded without hesitation.

Bailey could not wait to find out what this surprise was. She tried not to think that this would be her last memory with Nick and that they would never cross paths again. Her heartbeat was fierce as she let him continue to lead her out of the building and down the steps. She expected them to get into his limo or car at any moment; instead, he surprised her by walking past where the vehicles would have been parked. Her smile brightened as she knew where they were headed: the beach.

Nick led Bailey out further by the ocean shore, stopping momentarily to remove her platform shoes from her feet. "Sit, my love; I want you to feel the sand on your feet and be at peace with nature and our love." His soft-spoken words touched Bailey's heart, and tears of happiness and anguish threatened her eyes again. She pushed them back, took a deep breath, and sat on the warm sand. She reached up to remove her blindfold and removed her shoes at the soft touch of Nick's hands. She let out a small laugh when he stopped her.

"Sorry, my pet, but I want you to leave it on a bit longer. Seeing the ocean is one thing, but feeling it is far better," he teased. After removing Bailey's second shoe, Nick pulled her gently back up from the sand. The grainy texture messaged her bare feet. She sucked in a breath tasting the air in her lungs and letting it refresh her. He watched her facial expressions change with each step they took on the beach.

Nick was content watching Bailey's smile and feelings as the sand ticked her feet. He knew the memory of today would follow them for years to come. They would no doubt want to relive it every anniversary until they grew old together. "Dance with me," he asked in a strained voice that seduced her ears.

Bailey bit her lower lip, letting Nick take her tiny, trembling hands into his; no answer was needed. He knew she would dance with him always. The cool evening air circled them as they moved and swayed in perfect unison. The wind blowing swished Bailey's hair across her shoulders, casting a vision that would forever be branded in Nick's mind.

Bailey thought her heart would burst from all the love it experienced at that moment as they continued dancing, making a memory that would keep her alive and fighting until the end. She felt a single tear fall from her eye when he finally reached up and removed the blindfold. Their eyes locked; the raw emotion in his took her breath away. She felt her heart skip a beat as she tried to read his feelings.

"Bailey," Nick whispered hoarsely.

"Be my wife, marry me?"

Bailey almost burst into tears from all the love she could see in Nick's hazel eyes. Love for her and only her; she took his hand, letting him pull her into those strong arms again for the last time. Tears fell from her eyes; being his wife would make her the happiest woman in the world. She wanted to cry out to him, scream I can't, but she could not find the words. She knew it was a lie, but she felt her head nod and her small, cracked voice answering him with a shaky reply.

"yes."

Nick was relieved when he heard Bailey say yes. He kissed her deeply, madly tightening his hold around her body. Tonight, he would hold her naked in his arms all night to feel her skin on his skin. He loved her, and she loved him back. Everything was perfectly in place and at peace. He never thought he could ever feel as calm and content as he did at this moment, holding his future wife in his arms.

Later in the night, Nick passed out, and Bailey slipped from his arms. When she was sure she hadn't woke him, she dressed quickly. She knew Jewel would be there somewhere waiting for her answer and that she would waste no time in making her pain complete. She was relieved to find Kaitlyn wrapped tightly in a passed-out Jax's arms inside the hotel. Seeing how content they were together and how perfect they were together made her sure she was making the right choice. She kept them safe and happy with their son, and it was worth losing Nick.

Meanwhile, Jewel was growing impatient, pacing the floors, waiting for Bailey to come to her with her decision. She was about to go after her when she saw her walking into her room, a suitcase in her hands. An evil grin spread across her face. "I see you have made the right choice. Tell me how it feels," she taunted. From the tears in Bailey's eyes, she knew she was destroying her, so she smiled wider.

"At last, my once-time friend but now bitter enemy, you know how I felt when I lost Jax," Jewel said in a cruel, cold voice. The brutal words she spat at Bailey reminded her of a poem she had written when she lost Jax; the words rang like a bell. *Her true self she must now hide; no one can ever know of all the tears she has cried. She is forever lost; her warm heart has become as cold as frost. All they'll see are her lies, while on the inside, she cries, why can't they see or hear me? I am sheer misery!* She had written it at the lowest time in her disastrous life. She told Bailey they would be leaving tonight, so she could not say goodbye to any of them.

Bailey felt utterly numb from her head to her feet as she helped Jewel pack the rest of their bags. She had nothing before returning to Kaitlyn and Nick's lives, and now, she'd be leaving the same. Well, she told herself in silence, I won't be after all because she did have all the love Nick gave her deep inside her breaking heart. This knowledge alone branded her soul as the tears fell down her flushed cheeks. She did know one thing for sure: she would never forgive Jewel for this; she vowed to herself that she would make sure she had all she wanted from her and much more than she bargained for.

23

After packing all her things, Jewel told Bailey to follow her to a cab waiting outside the hotel to pick them up. A defeated Bailey did as she was commanded without a single word of refusal, knowing her fate had already been chosen and there was no going back now. She could only pray that Nick, Kaitlyn, and Jax would let her go and never come searching for her. "Goodbye, my only love. We may meet again in another world, goodbye to a friend's sister. Please take care of Kaitlyn and Nick," she whispered to the night.

Jewel glanced at Bailey, curious; she had never seen her look so lost and defeated, and for a very brief second, she nearly regretted making her leave Nick. The regret came to a sudden halt when she forced herself to remember how Jax told her to get lost, ignoring her tears and her vows of undying love for him. She remembered the birth of her daughter and how she had to give her up for adoption. With these memories, she became her bitter self once again.

"I must admit, I take pleasure in being the one to break you, to snatch away the man you love,' Jewel hissed. A cruel smile played on her lips; she knew her words would further shatter Bailey's spirit and reveled in it.

"Tell me, Jewel, don't you ever grow weary of your pathetic jealousy over losing Jax to his one true love, Kaitlyn," Bailey snapped, wanting to lash out at her. She was desperate to cause her a little bit of the pain she caused her. The problem is it backfired in her face.

"I will make it my life's mission to ensure you eat those words. When Nick finally replaces you with another, I'll be sure to run her in your nose as you have Kaitlyn in mine," Jewel snapped venomously.

The thought of Nick with another woman tore at Bailey's heart and shredded her soul. She realized she would never be able to get at Jewel the way she just got at her. She was utterly defeated, turning her head as she stared out the car window. She wanted to fire back and claim Nick would never replace her as Jax had her, but sadly, she knew it was invalid. Forever was a long time, and men got lonely-he would eventually find another.

Jewel was grateful that the past few years had taught her how to hide her genuine emotions. Bailey's words had cut her deep; everything she felt for Jax those two years back was still there and still very real. She knew that if her revenge was to be complete, she had to keep her guard up constantly. She reminded herself that emotions were easy to borrow when love was not a word that she had ever truly known from another. She desperately wished she could deny it but still cared a lot for Bailey. The problem was that she was consumed with bitterness and needed to take it out on any and everyone.

When Jewel thought of another cruel way to lash out at Bailey, she heard her snoring and looked up to see her fast asleep. She knew she could wake her but left it until the morning instead. Jewel also decided to take advantage of her foe's sleep and get some rest. She laid her head on the window glass, closed her heavy eyes, and let sleep fall over her.

Hours later, in a hotel room together, Jewel and Bailey sat on opposite beds. Jewel could not take the awkward silence, so she decided to tell Bailey how she and Jax originally met.

"Did I ever tell you how we met Bailey? How did I end up in Jax's bed to begin with? How he ended up like a brand in my heart and soul," she asked.

"No, but I am not sure it matters now, so why bother telling me at all, Bailey fired back.

"Of course, it wouldn't matter to you. You are far too selfish to care about anyone but yourself. Like it or not, it matters to me, even though I doubt you will understand the bond or connection between two broken souls like me and him," Jewel hissed in anger. Not waiting for another salty reply from Bailey, she began her story.

"I was a new dancer at the first club I ever worked at; the Seeds of Sorrow was looking for an exotic dancer for one of their big gigs. Jax was the band member there to seek out this dancer to go on tour with them and perform at the concert. Oh, Bailey, he was so handsome-a dark and dangerously handsome, the kind that consumes a woman inside and out. You can imagine my shock and excitement when he chose me; even with all those other more experienced dancers, he wanted me. We had this instant connection. I was broken, and he was slightly bent; we just fit. Our passions and fire synced together. I should have known where there was fire. It is inevitable that one of us will get burnt." Jewel stopped talking for a few fleeting moments as she let their memory slide across her mind.

"Jax had so many trust issues due to the hardships of his past and the undeniable reality that most who knew him only pretended he mattered for a chance at fame. I myself had much pride and fear of being used or abandoned. I was so afraid of being hurt by him that when his jealousy rose, I stupidly let him believe the worst of me. I let him think I slept with all of them, the entire band, after he had made love to me. My mistake drove a wedge between us that kept his deep feelings for me from growing or taking root deep enough to form any real between us. Jewel sighed with regret.

"So basically, you had an awful reputation, and so Jax was easily sold on the idea that you would screw anything. However, because you and he both had insatiable habits, he still kept you around for sex. Your ignorance of not defending the allegations against you pushed you two apart, but like a fool, you decided to remain his whore. What does any of this matter now," Bailey spat venomously.

"Like I said, you will never understand. The point is this: Jax and I had finally grown closer those few months after Kaitlyn broke his heart. Before you came and begged him to go after her. With a few more months, I know in my heart and soul that he and I would have become something far deeper than lovers," Jewel insisted.

"You are fucking delusional," Bailey shouted.

Jewel knew she could lash out at Bailey for her comments, but the truth was she got harder and smarter from all the rejections and pain of other's words and actions. She became harder from all the mental, physical, and emotional abuse made her the vindictive woman she is today. These were dark truths and secrets she would never tell anyone. She was fucked up, broken, and tired of being used. Even with all this, she was an extremely strong woman. She was built never to fall down. She would see them all on their knees before she admitted defeat.

"I cannot be blamed; my love for Jax made me crazy, I suppose," Jewel whispered more to herself than to Bailey.

"Everyone hurts. They just don't turn all their hurt into vengeance like you, Jewel. Do you not find your inability to forgive thick and suffocating? Why not seek redemption instead of this pointless revenge," Bailey asks.

"He ripped my heart out and left me to bleed, so, yes, I turned cold. I have gone to the extreme for my revenge. I do not want redemption, Bailey. I just wanted you to hear my story. When you have lived the type of life I've lived, it is pointless to try for any kind of peace or redemption. So, instead, I will take you all down the same road. I've ever known. In the end, you will see why I refused to change. From the moment I was born, I was chained to my fate- alone and wretched. Besides, I did you a favor anyhow, Bailey. Did I not tell you never to trust a Playboy? It is better to leave before you get left. Jax taught me this."

"No, Jewel. You have just put up so many walls that it's impossible for anyone to care. Love and hate have become twisted together for you. I want to understand, but... I would like to believe we could reconcile the past, but you keep burning down every bridge and everyone around you. It's not fair to deny me love because yours became destructive and void, and you know it. So, you can forget about telling me anything about your past and present because the love and respect that I once had for you is gone. I thought you should know this before you spill out any more shit that I no longer care about," Bailey shouts.

"That's fine, Bailey; I am here to always remind you of the mess that you left when you and Jax turned away from me. Did you truly believe you could just forget about me? You two being well and at peace was a slap to my face. How quickly I was replaced and betrayed was the most painful thing I've ever been through. I deserve this revenge, this vengeance, so yes, you are correct. There is no need to explain myself to you. We are not friends anymore. Hell, I doubt we ever truly were, to begin with", Jewel shouts back.

Bailey has nothing more to say, so she quietly gets up from bed and walks into the bathroom. She cannot stand to hear any more of Jewel's twisted truths. She decides to take a shower and wait to find out what horrid existence she has planned for her now. She becomes numb and unnaturally calm as she slides her clothes off and steps into the shower stall.

Jewel lets Bailey walk away, deciding it was truly pointless to try and justify her actions and emotions to someone as untainted or touched by life's harsher realities. She will let the little rich-spoiled rebel take her precious shower in peace tonight. Tomorrow, she would introduce her to her new reality. There will not be enough washing to make her feel truly clean after she brings her completely into her dark-erotic life. As she lies across her bed, she wonders if Bailey will be strong enough to survive what she has in store for her.

24

Nick woke up to find that his whole world had changed within a few hours. He was all alone in his bed, and Bailey was nowhere to be found. At first, he thought that perhaps she was with Kaitlyn somewhere around the hotel. This thought was quickly dismissed as he went inside to find Kaitlyn lying across Jax's chest, still fast asleep. Jax was awake, lying there smoking a cigarette.

"What's wrong," he asked.

"I was looking for Bailey. I proposed last night, and she said yes, but now I can't find her anywhere. Have you seen her," Nick asked anxiously.

"No, I haven't seen her since last night, but she can't be far. Congratulations, man."

After finding out Jax had not seen Bailey since last night, Nick said thanks to him and rushed off. He checked on the tour bus, hoping she was there with his whole heart. When he went inside, he started to panic, for she was nowhere to be found. His breathing became heavy; his heart began to hammer in his chest. Unwanted tears threatened to fill his eyes as reality was setting in. Bailey had left him, just walked out of his life without even saying goodbye or giving an explanation.

Why??

Nick's pain soon began to turn to a maddening rage until he slammed his fist into the wall of the bus. This only fed the fuel to the fire. He grabbed everything he bought her that she left behind, tore it all into tiny shreds, and then burnt it in the sink. As he watched it all burn, he felt empty, betrayed, and desperate to lash out at everyone, hell, anyone. He slammed his fists into the first person he saw, who happened to be Jax.

The moment Nick swung at him, Jax knew Bailey was gone, that she had walked out on him. He knew she must have snuck off as they all slept, which explained why Nick was so shocked. He understood that he needed to vent. He pushed him, almost knocking him over. "Come on and let it all out, man. Let it go. I can take it," he insisted.

Nick swung again, contacting Jax's nose, causing it to bleed slightly. He then kept on shoving Jax, hitting him in the chest and gut repeatedly. Again, Jax yelled at him.

"Come on, hit me harder, and let it out!"

Nick fell to his knees, shouting Bailey's name; tears fell down his cheeks. He continued yelling, cursing her name. Jax wiped his nose, spit blood from his mouth, and walked over to him, and in a voice of sheer concern, he spoke to him gentler.

"It will be all right. Just breathe, man. I am here; it's all right to cry, to feel."

Kaitlyn nearly passed out from shock when she saw Jax had let Nick hit him repeatedly without even flinching. It wasn't until Nick shouted Bailey's name and fell to his knees that she realized what was happening. She couldn't accept it, couldn't believe Bailey would not leave without even saying goodbye to her. With all this on her mind, she approached them to argue that Bailey must have an explanation for her rash actions.

"Damn it, Kaitlyn, it's not up to us whether or not Nick decides to look for Bailey," Jax shouted in an irritated tone.

"Fine, then I will find her and to hell with the consequences. She is my only friend, Jax Alan. I love her!" Jax hated it when Kaitlyn got like this; he knew he had no choice but to try to convince Nick to look for Bailey. He knew she would never let it rest if he didn't.

Nick finished loading the tour bus to leave, needing any distraction from the unbearable pain in his heart. It felt like the knife had been pierced and twisted into his gut, leaving his heart to bleed out for all eternity. Hearing Jax and Kaitlyn shouting at one another, he stopped packing and decided to see what was happening. When he found out, he decided to go after Bailey, even if only to let her know how much pain she had caused him. Perhaps to find a way to inflict the same pain upon her heart as she had his. With those thoughts, he went back out to the bus and finished.

25

Kaitlyn tried desperately to understand how Bailey could do something like this. She knew she loved Nick, and there was no reason to leave him, not until he finally loved her back. "There has to be some logical reason for Bailey leaving us like that; there just has to be. I don't care if you disagree, Jax, so you better not say otherwise around me," she said irritated. She hated it when he looked at her like he knew better than her what was happening around them. She knew he did not mean to do it, but he always had that look, especially now.

Jax looked deeply into Kaitlyn's grey eyes, wishing she could be right now. Wishing he could also believe what she had convinced herself about Bailey. The thing was, he knew how wild and careless Bailey was in the past. To him, it seemed she had not changed much; after all, she was indeed a stripper. He wished he could just help Kaitlyn, and Nick let her go and forget her, move on because she would. He hated seeing the two of them so hurt over that little cheap lying whore.

By the sparkle in his eyes, Kaitlyn knew that Jax thought Bailey knew precisely what she was doing and meant to do it. He more than likely thought she wanted revenge and came after it, not caring who it crushed in the end. This angered her to the core; she glared at him. Then she thought perhaps these were her thoughts, not his. Why, she thought silently, would Bailey want to hurt her like this? Did she hold a grudge for her leaving her behind those two terrible years ago?

Jax knew by heavy tears streaming down Kaitlyn's beautiful face that she needed his comfort and support, so he gently pulled her into his strong arms. "I will do whatever it takes to find

Bailey. I will bring her back here if I can. I love you, Kaitlyn, and I will do anything to help you with this. I hate when you are hurting; it kills me," he soothed. He hated seeing the woman he loved like this, in so much pain. He wished he could face Bailey now, strangle her for coming back into their lives, only hurt them in some twisted revenge game.

Nick sat back, watching Kaitlyn crying in Jax's arms over losing Bailey, and he became twice as bitter towards her. He knew how much she meant to Kaitlyn; she was like her sister. Kaitlyn loved her just as much as he did. He decided to do whatever it took to find Bailey and did not care if it took a lifetime. He was going to make her face the pain she had caused them, make her feel it tenfold. She would face his wrath as it burned like the flaming fires of hell.

26

IT HAD BEEN TWO MONTHS since Bailey walked out on Nick, Kaitlyn, and little Tristen. She felt so empty inside. Jewel forced her to get a job with her at some low-grade, sleazy strip.

The club where she was part owner was called the Pleasure Seeker. Each night, they both performed together on the stage, and each time she danced with Jewel, she wanted to choke the life from her body. The pain she felt deep inside kept her awake at night, like she could hear Nick calling her to him. His heart shouted that she belonged to him as if he belonged to her. *Just come back to me, it echoed in her ears. Everything will be all right;* she felt so lost, so defeated, broken, just beaten, that she had become numb inside. Several nights, she wanted to lock herself up in her dressing room and cry the night away. Never once before winning Nick's love had she felt ashamed when she danced naked on a stage that all had changed now. She felt like a piece of meat to be passed around to anyone who wanted a taste. She could not figure out why she felt this way for the rest of her life. Perhaps his love purified her once sin-filled soul.

Nick stood in the back of The Pleasure Seeker strip club, waiting for Bailey to dance. He learned from a good band buddy that she began working here a little over a month ago. He could not believe he waited two months for this moment to do whatever it took to hurt her like she had him. He felt nothing but despair and endless rage since she walked from his life. A rage that seemed to consume all the human emotions within him. He swore he would make her pay for causing him to love her so completely. He would make her suffer for walking out on him as if he

meant nothing to her at all.

Bailey finished fixing her makeup and put a fake smile on her face. She walked out onto the stage, letting the music in the club and the bright lights of the stage take her to another world. She began to shake her body to the beat of the music. Jewel danced with her, feeling proud of all she had done to destroy her. In return, Bailey looked into Jewel's eyes to see how in control she felt, which sickened her.

Nick's heart hammered when he saw how beautiful Bailey was that night. She was wearing a red velvet corset with fishnet pantyhose. Her firm, round, perky breasts almost burst from the top of her corset. Her blond hair hung in tiny braids, and on her lips, she wore light pink lipstick, which made her lips glow in the light of the stage. Her corset revealed her round ass and its firmness for all eyes in the club to see and fantasize about. The realization of this caused a stab of jealousy to shoot through his body. He smiled in pleasure and jealousy when she almost fell from the stage, seeing him in the back of the crowd. He stared straight at her, their eyes locked instantly, letting her see all his raw emotions shining through his glare.

Bailey could see Nick's pain, rage, confusion, and jealousy mixed in his dark eyes. Her heart nearly burst from her chest with sheer agony, for she, too, felt the same pain. He looked so devastatingly handsome even now when things between them were so messed up. She panicked, wondering what Jewel would do now that he had found her. She ran from the stage back to her dressing room. She had to get away from him before he confronted her, which would cause Jewel to change her mind about destroying Kaitlyn.

Nick pushed his way past the crowd towards the club's dressing rooms. He had to get to Bailey before she was lost to him again. The club's bouncer stopped him until the guy realized who he was, and then he was let pass. He ran the rest of the way to the room that said Legs on it; finding it locked, he kicked the door open and stormed inside to see Bailey's eyes growing wide with fear. She tried to go past him back out of the door, but he caught her roughly by the arm.

"You are unbelievable, Bailey! I would have sacrificed everything if I could have made our dreams the same. But here you are, still running from me," he shouted in her face as she cried out in pain from the tight grip he had on her.

Fire was in Nick's eyes, determination in his jaw as he studied her face, gazing into her eyes. Bailey trembled under his scrutiny, unafraid of him but alarmed by her attraction to him. "Please, Nick, do not do this. You have to let me go," she begged. They stood staring into each other's eyes for what felt like an eternity when he finally pulled her closer.

"I hunger to hold you, kiss you, and make love to you even when I should hate you. I ache for you to return and complete me because you are my other half, Bailey." Nick's words touched Bailey's soul.

Nick's touch sent shivers down Bailey's spine. She felt her knees grow weak, and she wilted in his embrace. She needed him as he needed her, craved his kiss and caress as he craved to give them to her. He lowered his lips softly down upon hers, his teeth nibbled at her bottom one, and it trembled in passion. His lips continued to meet hers again and again. He held her, and she clung to him.

Nick knew Bailey was the missing half of his soul; whether he wanted to admit it or not, he had known it since he first met her years ago. He wanted her so badly that his hands were shaking as he caressed her passionate, swollen breasts and then her firm bottom. He needed to make love to her to breathe to live. He wanted to remind her how perfectly their bodies fit together and that they were one and always would be, no matter how hard she tried to fight it. He slid his hand up inside the bottom of her corset, stroking her tender flesh between her trembling thighs. She moaned against his lips. Nick bent down to take one nipple in his mouth, sucking and teasing with his tongue and teeth, toying with her sensitive flesh.

Bailey gripped Nick's shoulder and moaned his name in half plea and half surrender. He suckled her, his warm hand caressing her secret region, causing her to burn for him. Bailey's senses began to reel. She wanted him so bad it hurt, and her body ached with need. A need she could no longer fight. She ran her hand savagely through his hair.

"Please stop this, Nick, stop before we do something we will regret," she whispered desperately. She tried to push his hand away from her burning nether region," she cried reluctantly-desperately. Nick quickened his caress, causing her to nearly burst into flames of desire, hot as the fires of hell. Bailey couldn't do this with him now, not ever; she had to protect Kaitlyn no matter what. She could not give in to her body or her heart. As she fought him, Nick backed her against the dressing room table. Before she could even blink an eye, he lifted her on top of it.

Nick would not let Bailey push him away, not now, not this time. He tore the front of her corset, exposing more than her taunt nipples to his caresses. With a sigh, he lowered his mouth to suckle them once more, using his teeth again to nibble at her tender flesh. His free hand tore the rest of her corset to touch the bare, sensitive flesh of her inner thighs. He would make her crave him just as he craved her so that in the end, she would be begging him to take her home with him to be his wife.

Bailey felt her body begin to lose all control, mainly when Nick thrust his fingers deep within her warm-seeking body. She instinctively spread her thighs wider, throwing her head back to give his mouth better access to her aching breasts. With each agonizing thrust of his fingers, her body shook uncontrollably until she burst free in sheer pleasure. Her body showered his warm fingers with its sweet moister. She gasped as he dropped to his knees before her and nuzzled the flat of her quivering stomach. His hands caressed her bottom and skimmed over her hips. His mouth followed; she again ran her hands frantically through his hair to urge him further.

Nick smiled at Bailey and her passion-filled eyes as she pulled him up from tasting her sweetness.

Bailey sat up frantically, releasing his aching shaft from his pants. "Nick, make love to me; take me now," she begged.

Nick pulled her down to the edge of the dresser, wrapping her legs around his thighs where, in one solid thrust, he entered her tight, warm, eager body. He swore he could die from the sweet torture her body inflicted upon his own. He loved Bailey madly and wanted to show her by making love to her every night for the rest of her life. He needed her to enjoy this as much as he did, no matter the cost.

Tears ran down Bailey's face as she felt Nick's shaft fill her body. She wanted to be his wife and tell him the truth, but she knew this was impossible. She knew she would have to say goodbye for good this time. She knew now that she had made love with him. It would be that much harder on them both. It would devastate him to the very core. She honestly did not know how she was going to survive losing him again. She should have never let him touch her. This would be a brand they would never forget—a scar they will both bear for the rest of their lives.

After making love to her three times, Nick spoke to Bailey. "Come back with me. It doesn't matter why you left as long as you never leave me again. I love you, Bailey. I refuse to live without you. Marry me?" Bailey pulled out of his arms and quickly began to dress, then she turned to face him again, crying.

"Nick, please forgive me. Forget this happened tonight; forget me," she begged. The darkness of his eyes told her he was angry and that forgiveness would be impossible. She hated leaving things so wrong between them.

"I have to do this to protect Kaitlyn and Jax. If you love me as you claim, you will let me go and try to understand what I do is out of love."

Nick listened to all of Bailey's words before finally losing his temper, slamming his fist into the mirror of her dresser. "I will go, but remember that I own your heart and soul and will never let it go. I will never forgive you for making me leave you like you left me. You can go straight to hell. The same hell you have sent me, too," he hissed.

Bailey wanted to die, and he then turned and walked away from her forever. She watched Nick walk away before falling to her knees, crying his name. She cried until her face went numb, and her eyes became swollen. Her heart felt like it was shattering into a million tiny pieces; it even hurt to breathe. She closed her eyes tight, rocking back and forth, wishing death would come for her and end this misery.

27

Jax looked up to see a furious Nick storming in his direction, "What happened with Bailey? I know you went after her?"

"I found her. I cried. She cried. We made love, and then she dismissed me again, saying she had to do this to protect you and Kaitlyn. What the hell did she mean by that? If you know something, Jax, tell me now!" Nick demanded, looking deep into his eyes, where he saw in them that Jax knew something. The question was, what was it, and how bad was it? Nick knew he should have known something fishy with Jax these past two years. Honestly, he was dreading the answer he now waited to hear.

Jax always knew this day would come. He was relieved because he had grown weary of living with his secret. He was glad Kaitlyn was not there to have to relive it all. He motioned with his hand for Nick to sit down. "I am about to tell you a very long story that I will never forget. An event which has weighed heavy on my mind for a very long time." As Jax told his story, he left out no details.

"Kaitlyn's father was harboring a dark secret. It turned out he wasn't even her father. I swear, Nick, the events of the night haunt my dreams. The way I found Kaitlyn, how lifeless she looked on that bed. That pig beat her, tried to rape her, a woman he raised from an infant. He came at me with a knife, there was a struggle, and he, umm, I accidentally killed him," Jax's voice drifted, hot tears streamed down his face.

By the time Jax finished his horrible tale, Nick realized why Bailey wanted to protect Kaitlyn because he did, too. He felt the same about Jax and Tristen as Bailey did Kaitlyn. The only thing he could not figure out was what leaving him had to do with protecting them. Then it hit him like a ton of pure lead. Jewel. He remembered seeing her sneaking around the night Bailey disappeared on him; somehow, she must have discovered what happened in Druid Hills. Jewel must have used it to blackmail Bailey. It finally made sense to him how she must blame Bailey for Jax going after Kaitlyn and wanting to punish her.

"I am going after Bailey again. I will find a way to make it work for us all, to protect you and your family and still be with Bailey," Nick swore, and without hearing Jax's reply, he ran from the room.

Jax figured out what happened, too. Jewel wanted her revenge on him for tossing her aside for Kaitlyn. He knew he had to find Kaitlyn and tell her Jewel knew everything, that it was time to turn himself in. He was terrified of losing her and their son, but he knew it was the only way to give Nick a chance to have the happiness he had with Kaitlyn these past two years. What he regretted the most was how Kaitlyn would react to his arrest. He knew he was her entire world, and she lived for him as he lived for her.

When she looked into Jax's stormy eyes, Kaitlyn knew what he would say. She could see their fear, pain, and desperation. Tears sprang to her eyes. "Jax, please don't. Let's run the three of us, you, me, and our son," she begged.

"If I run, I give up everything that makes me the man you fell in love with. I can't do that, Kaitlyn. If I walk away from the band, the life we have built together here, I am as good as dead. It's time to stop hiding, baby. I am just going to have to hope that the police believe us. I love you, Kaitlyn, and I have watched you sacrifice enough because of my actions that night." Jax let the tears fall as she threw herself in his arms and started crying.

"Make love to me here and now, please, one last time before I lose you," Kaitlyn begged.

The pain Jax saw in her beautiful eyes tore at his soul. He kissed the tears from her face, his tongue tasting her flesh. She wrapped her arms tightly around his neck, desperate to be as close to Jax as possible. His lips trailed from her tear-stained cheeks to her trembling lips, leaving soft kisses until his tongue slid into her mouth, caressing hers.

Jax swore Kaitlyn had never tasted this sweet; he needed her to sustain his fear of losing everything they cared about, losing their son. He groaned when he felt her small, warm hand slide down his pants and stroke his cock. Her hand was shaky but never once stopped its caress, causing his shaft to become rigid with need. Jax stopped kissing her lips and began to nibble at her neck and shoulders. "Undo my jeans, touch me, baby. Help me to give you what you desire," he groaned hoarsely.

Desperate to touch her man, Kaitlyn did as Jax asked. She unbuttoned his jeans and removed his hardened shaft from the confines of them. She bit her lip, running her hand up and down his length. Jax ripped her shirt, letting her breasts spring forth with his teeth. He scrapped her nipples, causing her to cry out when they turned into stiff peaks of raw desire. She knew if she lost him, this would be a night that kept her from losing her sanity. She knew that he was going to take her to the very edge of life and death with this lovemaking, letting out all. His fear, love, sadness, anger, as well as desires for her ever so willing body. She ran her hands through his unruly hair, her silent way of begging him for more. Her strokes on his shaft turn desperate. They became demanding squeezes as a fire as hot as a candle's flame raged within her.

Jax became a burning flame of raw emotion when Kaitlyn's caresses turned frantic upon his pulsating erection. He scooped her into his strong arms and sat her on a dresser in the room. He lowered his head between her opened thighs, using his tongue to send shivers all through her body.

"Jax, my love, I must feel your fingers inside my body. Please, please, give me what my body is bleeding for," Kaitlyn begged as the caresses of Jax's tongue on her secret region caused her to burn like the fires of hell. She swore she could not get enough of him to suit her. She wanted to make this a night they would carry with them for the rest of their lives.

Jax thrust his fingers gently, then savagely into Kaitlyn's hot, hungry body, giving her what she begged him to give. As he withdrew and then entered over and over again, he bit her inner thigh gently yet firmly, causing her to drench his hand with her body's sweetness. The feel of her body's release nearly sent him over the edge. "Show me what you will miss when I am gone, baby," he growled.

Kaitlyn sat on the dresser and slid off to lower to her knees. She left kisses along the entire length of Jax's throbbing shaft, teasing him. When she heard him suck in a breath of pleasure, she opened her mouth to taste him. She swore nothing tasted as good as he did at that very second.

"Enough," Jax demanded as he pulled Kaitlyn to her feet and kissed her savagely, scrapping her bottom lip with his teeth, causing it to bleed. The taste of her blood on his tongue was bittersweet. He lifted her to wrap her legs around his muscular thighs.

"Jax." Kaitlyn cried as he slammed her against the wall, thrusting his shaft deep within her boiling-in-desired body. She bit down on his neck with her teeth as the thrusting of his shaft sent her spinning into eternal bliss. Jax smiled, looked deep into her eyes, and spoke demands of passion.

"Scream for me, Kaitlyn! Tell me how much you like it when I take you like this. How much you love me."

"I love you. You are my husband in every way that matters. No other man will touch me like this. No man but you will ever have my heart or body, I swear," Kaitlyn cried. After hearing her passion speak vows that no other man would ever have her body, Jax buried his head in her damp hair. His pulsating cock spilled its hot seed deep within her womb.

The feel of Jax's warm, welcomed seed caused Kaitlyn to shake all over, and her juices came forth, showering his shaft that still pumped within her. After quenching their bodies' thirst several times, leaving them swollen and soar, they slid to the floor and held each other as if it would be the last time. They knew that the fact was he killed a man who was thought of as her father. A man who had been a respected preacher and with no proof that he hurt her except her scars, Jax's chances of being let off in self-defense were slim.

28

BAILEY STOOD FROZEN in time as Jewel scolded her. "I know you made love with Nick. I should expose Jax because of your ignorance. I should hurt your dearest Kaitlyn for your betrayal. I suppose I will just let you make it up to me instead. I'll let it slide if you agree to take my place as a trick tonight."

"No," Bailey cried... "I am not a whore, and I never will be. Please do not ask me to do this!" Her pleas went unnoticed.

Jewel refused to back down or take no for an answer. "The guy is an overnight client; he is harmless. He likes it a little rough but nothing dangerous. Besides, it's the only way I will continue to keep Kaitlyn and Jax's dirty secret."

Bailey realized she had no choice, so she stopped pleading and slipped into one of Jewel's skin-tight black dresses and fishnet pantyhose. "This is a one-time thing, Jewel. I will never do this again. After it's over, I am leaving California, and you will have the ultimate revenge on me," Bailey sobbed.

Jewel knew Bailey's words were valid, so she nodded in a silent yes. Her way of silently telling Bailey she would let her go. The revenge she took on her did not feel so good anymore. It did not fill the void of losing Jax and their secret love child that constantly filled her heart.

Hours later, after begging and pleading with Jewel to at least accompany her to this john's place, she and Jewel knocked on the guy's door. He answered quickly. When they walked into this man's home, Bailey felt very uneasy. Everywhere she looked, there were chains, whips, and other torture devices. The man had an empty, evil glare in his dark, soulless eyes.

Bailey could tell by the surprised look on Jewel's face that she lied about the man being a regular. He was a new client. She had no real idea what he might be into or what he might do to them. Bailey wanted to run but knew she could not leave Jewel here alone even if she were just as evil as this man might be. The thing was, she once loved Jewel very much, and she refused to let anything wrong happen to her.

Jewel smiled at the man as sweetly as she could, "I will lower the price, and you can have us both tonight if you accompany us back to my hotel," she asked calmly. After a few hesitant moments, the john reluctantly agreed, following them. This helped relieve some uneasiness they felt about this man. He was just too quiet, too relaxed yet alert to be trusted. They were terrified of what he might have done if they used his apartment as he requested. When they entered the hotel room next to Jewel's, the man told them to remove their clothes and get on nothing but pantyhose and high heels.

Bailey followed Jewel's lead, shedding her clothing. She went to her knees. She shook all over with unease at this strange request. Her shivering increased when she heard him sliding off his belt; then, before she saw it coming, he grabbed her wrists. He tied them tightly behind her back with the belt. The leather cut into her delicate flesh, and she cried out in pain.

"I don't want to do this anymore; let me go now," Bailey cried. Jewel looked over to her. The fear she saw in her eyes became her own.

"Stop this, stop it all, and let us both go. This was not part of the arrangement we made over the phone," Jewel shouted.

The john grabbed Bailey up by her hair, dragging her to the bed. He threw her down hard onto the mattress. She struggled when she heard Jewel arguing with him again to release them both, and he laughed. She watched in horror as Jewel jumped to her feet, hitting and screaming at him for hurting her.

Bailey's eyes grew wide in fear as she watched this maniac slap Jewel so brutally that she fell back onto the marble table. Her head hit the hard surface with a sickening crack, killing her instantly. Bailey screamed and rolled from the bed, trying to run from this terrible place to get help. She just knew she was going to die just like Jewel, that he would not let her live to be a witness to his crime. She felt him grab her by her hair, pulling her back against him. He said many vile things to her while unbuttoning his pants with his free hand, pulling his shaft out.

Once again, the man dragged Bailey over to the bed, where he again threw her violently, pouncing on top of her. He slapped her hard across the face, splitting her lip. She just lay there crying hysterically while he continued to hit her again and again. She tried to kick at him when she felt him tare at her pantyhose. He grabbed her already bound wrists, tying them to the bedpost with her torn pantyhose.

"NO. Please, God, NO," Bailey screamed as he then tied her feet. Wanting to be anywhere but there, she closed her tear-filled eyes and thought of Nick. She thought of his love for her and how he treated her gently. She needed this love now to help her escape from the rough, vile hands of this maniac grabbing at her tender, bruised flesh. She passed out cold, feeling the maniac bite deep into her flesh, drawing blood. The agonizing pain it inflicted on her tender body was just too much for her to handle. Right before passing out, Nick's face popped into her mind.

29

Meanwhile, back where Kaitlyn and Jax were, the police had Jax in handcuffs after taking his confession of killing the Minister two years ago. Kaitlyn watched in sheer agony, knowing she could do nothing to stop them. Her eyes locked with Jax's, and she grabbed his shirt, pulling him into a kiss. A kiss filled with a passion that even Heaven would perish in comparison to. Her lips left him to leave a trail of kisses along his jawline; tears ran down her cheeks.

"I love you, Jax. No matter what, I love you," Kaitlyn whispered. The police asked her to accompany them downtown to give her a statement. She nodded and followed the other officer to his car after Jax told her he loved her and that she would be safe. As the officer led her away, she wondered how she would ever live without him.

Not quite an hour later, once the officer had him in a secure room, he uncuffed Jax and asked him to give his statement about that night. Jax closed his eyes, letting his memory of that night flow back into his head. He saw Kaitlyn lying on that bed, looking lifeless. Once again, he felt rage so intense that he nearly shouted out the same thing he had to her father before ending his worthless life. He remembered how afraid he had been when thinking he had already lost her and how helpless he felt that he had not gotten there sooner that night. He broke down crying and began telling his story immediately, leaving out nothing.

"I was at a concert about to go out on stage when Bailey came to me and told me Kaitlyn had been taken by her father. I admit I should have gone to the police but was too frantic to get to her. She told me many times how her father abused her. I boarded my jet and went after her. When I got there, I didn't knock. I broke in and found her father crazy-eyed and praying nonsense about the devil and his whore. I asked for Kaitlyn, and he kept spouting nonsense, so I threw him aside and proceeded up the stairs, shouting her name. I found her in a bed upstairs beaten, and I admit I saw red that I wanted to kill him. I returned to him with bad intentions; he came at me, we struggled, and he fell wrong. The weapon he yielded hit him exactly right, and it killed him. I rushed back, woke her, and confessed everything to her. She told me she was carrying my child, and I panicked. I know it was wrong, but I can't deny that I have no regret that he is dead. I admit I wanted him to be, but not at my hand."

After listening to Jax's side of this monstrous tale, the officer knew he was not lying. He honestly believed he would have done the same had it been his wife and her father. He hoped Kaitlyn's tale matched his, and he could get some evidence to prove that the man had been violent and wasn't even her actual father. He left the room after Jax finally calmed down enough to be trusted alone. He had to get Kaitlyn's story and discover what she had suffered at the minister's dark hands.

Kaitlyn glanced up at the officer as he entered the room, "where is Jax? Is he all right," she asked.

"Jax is all right, Kaitlyn. He is at another end of the building. Listen, I need you to tell me what happened the night your father died?"

"He was not my father; he was an evil, lying psychopath who tried to kill me," Kaitlyn shouted. The officer saw raw fear in her eyes as she let her memory take her back in time. He felt pity for her having to rehash the most terrifying night of her life. He listened to her, watching her eyes change from fear to sadness, then back to fear, until she finally finished her gruesome tale. He watched silently as she stood, raising her shirt to reveal the deep scar that trailed down her back. He knew every word they said was accurate when he saw that scar. The Minister had a dark, devious side that he hid very well.

"We will want a blood test to confirm the minister was honest when he revealed that he wasn't your father. I promise we will do everything to track down his wife and get her side of the story. We will try to find concrete evidence that the minister tried to kill the both of you." the officer vowed.

Kaitlyn closed her eyes, praying to the Gods above that the officer could find proof to release Jax. She ached with fear for him and their son. With her entire heart, she wished that Bailey was there for her. She desperately needed her friend to reassure her that it would be all right. The officer told her she could go for now, but she refused to leave Jax alone. She told him he would have to arrest her if he tried to make her go and that she would fight tooth and nail. She was relieved when he told her she could stay the night on the lounge couch and that he would do everything possible to see Jax released by dawn.

To Jax, morning drifting into evening drug on like an eternity; he ached to take Kaitlyn in his arms and reassure her that they would make it through this as a family. He smiled as he recalled the officer saying how she refused to leave there without him and that she threatened to throw a fit. He prayed for the first time, praying that the officer would find the evidence he sought. He knew that if he were not released, he would be so good as dead. The loss of his son and woman would destroy him. Jax paced so long and hard that exhaustion took over, and he fell into a deep sleep on his bunk.

It was a sunny day on the beach back home in California. Jax found himself walking barefoot in the sand; the soft, moist texture of the beach tickled at his feet. The salty smell of the ocean water filled his nostrils as the light breeze blew his hair across his face. There were tiny white and red roses on the sand leading to a destination unknown to him at this time. He followed these roses for a short distance, and there was another shift in the wind. His nostrils flared at the sweet scent of almonds and honey. His eyes shot straight ahead to see Kaitlyn, his breath caught in his throat.

Kaitlyn was standing at the end of the rose trail. She wore a wedding gown of pure antique lace. Jax's eyes scanned her dress from her breast to her bare feet. They trailed back up to her face, thinking she was simply breathtaking, too beautiful for words, with her long hair in a twist-like bun with tiny ringlets framing her face. She wore roses and pearls in her hair. Her eyes locked with his, and she smiled. Jax walked faster, his heart hammered. He could not wait to marry her. After a few long strides, he was at her side, taking her in his arms. He kissed her tenderly....

Jax woke up alone in a cell; tears trailed down his face. His heart became heavy. He wanted his dream to be a reality. He wanted to marry Kaitlyn and spend the rest of his life as her husband.

Later that night, the police officer approached Jax and told him he was being released. Jax looked at him in confusion. "How is that possible?" he asked.

The officer told Jax they went back to her alleged father's home. Inside the house, they began finding a secret room in his church. Inside the church was where they discovered a written plan to kidnap Kaitlyn from her college dorms and how he would cover up her death. Jax's face went as white as a ghost. He grew sick to his stomach, knowing that the monster had planned it all months before taking Kaitlyn. The officer went on to explain how they also contacted the wife, who told them he had beaten her a few days earlier and was always an evil, vindictive man who hid behind the lord to do as he wished. She confessed that he always had some strange obsession with Kaitlyn.

Jax was relieved that the evidence cleared him so he could be with his family again. He could now marry Kaitlyn like he always wanted to, and they could have the life they genuinely wanted together. He was released after signing tons of paperwork and answering a few questions. When Kaitlyn saw him leave that building, she ran to him, throwing herself into his arms. He squeezed her tightly in his strong arms, telling her how much he loved her.

"Kaitlyn, you are my life. I want to be your husband if you will have me. Kaitlyn, will you do me the honor of being my wife?"

Kaitlyn began to cry, nodding her head yes. Speechless, she passionately kissed Jax, her whole heart shuttered in her chest. Jax kissed her back, meeting passion with passion; he could hardly wait to get her home and make love to her. He hoped Nick would find Bailey and return soon. He could hardly wait to tell them that nothing stands in their way of happiness and that they can ask Jewel to go to hell.

30

Nick got Jewel's address after having to bribe the owner of The Pleasure Seeker strip club. He knew she would be the key to finding Bailey and setting everything straight. All he would have to do was find a way to get her to back off and move on. He had to convince her to keep her mouth shut about Kaitlyn and her father. Only then could he be with the woman he loved. He just hoped he could get through to her. He knew how stubborn and devious she could be. Jewel had always been a very inconsistent woman, selfish to the very core.

Nick kicked the door open when he got to Jewel's apartment, hoping to catch her off guard. Instead, he found her gone, and on her table was a crumbled address to a hotel on the floor. He took a deep breath and hoped to see her at this address.

A half hour or so later, Nick knocked at the door of the address on Jewel's table. He quickly found the hotel and her room because it was next to her old strip club. He knocked twice more, but there was no answer. He heard a few strange noises and decided Jewel was trying to hide. He kicked in the door, uncaring if the hotel sued him. He entered and was caught off guard when a man grabbed him by the throat, slamming him against the wall. Nick's eyes frantically scanned the room. He struggled to free himself from this man's firm grip. He soon found Jewel's lifeless body lying on the floor in a puddle of blood. He knew instantly this man had killed her. He slammed his head into the man's nose, sending him to his knee. He kicked him in the rib cage to make sure he stayed down.

Nick looked across the room and saw her, Bailey. She was tied to the bedpost. He was distracted by her beaten form and caught off guard again. He felt a sharp stab in his ribs, and he stumbled back into the now-closed door. The man tried to use this as a chance to run. Nick dove at him so hard that he knocked him over into the television set, which knocked him unconscious.

Nick lay against the door, letting everything that had happened sink into his mind. He felt numb all over, trying to figure out what happened here. He remembered Bailey that she was tied to the bed. He was afraid to go to her, terrified that, like Jewel, she was already dead.

Nick finally forced himself to go to her anyway because he loved her enough to ensure she was not. What he saw once he approached her made him sick to his stomach and tore at his heart, perhaps even his soul. He knew by the teeth marks on her flesh and the thousands of bruises that she had more than likely been raped. He frantically freed her bound hands and feet, then covered her naked body.

"Bailey, my love, it's me, baby, Nick. Please wake up. I am here now, and no one will ever hurt you like this again. I swear this to you," Nick cried, tears falling from his eyes. He continued to try to wake her until there was a call on the phone. He answered it, telling the person to call the police. It was the hotel manager, and he told him he would call then and there. When Nick hung up the phone, Bailey slowly began to open her eyes.

Bailey glanced up at Nick, thinking she was either dead or dreaming. Once she realized it was neither, she threw her arms around his neck and cried fiercely. She cried for all the things she had just been through. She shook from the shame she felt in getting herself into this mess. She gasped at all the love she saw in Nick's eyes.

The police arrived shortly after the manager's call to find Jewel's lifeless body on the floor and the suspect coming too. They quickly acted, pouncing on him. There was a struggle, and the suspect got one of the guns, forcing them to open fire on him. Justice had been served as the lunatic fell to his death next to Jewel's cold body. The paramedics went to Bailey to assist her. She was still wrapped tight in Nick's arms, and tears fell from her eyes.

"Nick, please take me out of here. Just take me home," Jewel begged. Nick looked at her, and it wounded his heart.

"Bailey, I will take you anywhere you wish, but you must let the paramedics look you over. I love you and swear never to let anything happen to you again," he promised.

The paramedics told her she needed to go with them to a hospital and that Nick could come if she wanted him to be there with her. As they loaded her into the ambulance, Nick promised her.

He would help her forget everything that happened to her tonight, even if it took all their lives to do so. He promised to kiss away all her tears and make her his wife. Tears fell from his emotion-filled eyes as he made a vow after vow.

Bailey knew Nick meant it. She raised her trembling hand and caressed his cheek. "Just seeing your eyes already healed my soul. Simply knowing you love me erased this nightmare," she whispered. He kissed the palm of her hand and let the ambulance take her.

Later that night, after having several tests run, Bailey sat in her hospital bed with Nick again at her side. Her body shook as he washed the blood from her bruised face since she refused to let anyone else touch her. She trusted him and knew he would never hurt her and would always be gentle and loving with her. She stood so he could slide what was left of her dress from her body, and the shaking subsided. He pulled her into his strong arms, kissing her gently on her forehead.

After cleaning the rest of Bailey's fragile body, Nick laid down beside her on her bed, causing her to at last fall fast asleep. He would stay up all night if he had to so that she could feel safe. He watched her with tears falling from his eyes at the realization of how close he had come to losing her. He could never describe the intense relief he felt when the Doctors confirmed that she had not been raped. He kissed her forehead, slid down in the hospital bed closer to her, and forced his own eyes to close. He drifted in and out of sleep, vowing tomorrow would be a better day.

The next day, Nick and Bailey walked out of the hospital, away from all the horrifying things that had happened to her the night before. As they walked hand in hand, she knew she would no longer be in a nightmare without escape. Her life would be full of love and contentment once she became his wife. He would give her the world. She smiled when she saw Jax and Kaitlyn waiting for them outside. Nick had called them that night after she had fallen asleep, explaining everything that had happened. In return, Jax told Nick how he turned himself in for the death of the reverend and was released due to lack of evidence.

Bailey was relieved they would all be together again, this time for good. She threw her arms around Kaitlyn. "I love you and miss you so much, Kaitlyn. I wish I could have told you the truth when Jewel blackmailed me," Bailey cried. Kaitlyn's tight hug and a soft kiss on her cheek told Bailey she forgave and loved her just as deeply.

EPILOGUE

It had been over a year since that horrifying night when she had nearly been raped as well as lost her life. Thanks to Nick and Kaitlyn, Bailey could barely remember any of it now. The love they gave her simply erased the trauma. She no longer had nightmares of that maniac or of Jewel being killed. Her life had become full of nothing but happiness, sheer bliss. Nick showered her with so much attention that it washed away her shame and disgrace. She looked into her full-length mirror to see her beautiful off white wedding gown and veil. Tears almost sprang forth from her eyes. When she thought of all the love and joy in her life, she fought the tears back and smiled at Kaitlyn, who was helping her finish getting ready.

As her maid of honor, Kaitlyn wore a forest green dress; her ready-to-give-birth-any-day-now abdomen stood out in contrast. Pregnancy gave her a luminous glow, making her all the more beautiful. Bailey hoped she would be as attractive as her when she carried her and Nick's first child. She glanced down to see the diamond-incrusted wedding band on Kaitlyn's finger from her wedding only a few months ago.

After talking to Kaitlyn for a while longer, Bailey finally began to walk down the aisle. As she walked, she locked eyes with the man she knew she would spend eternity with. She knew instantly by the sparkle in Nick's brown eyes that he was as anxious for their wedding night as she was.